My name's Nate Montgomery, and as a partner at Dillard, Collins, Montgomery and Associates, I have the best view of Chicago, my reputation is impeccable, and...well, I don't have to sit at home on a Friday night unless I want to. All things to envy, sure, but still no reason for someone to blackmail me!

I called in Rennie Paris, a private investigator who's done outstanding work for me for two years. Little did I know this was where my trouble would really start.

I always thought Rennie was plain, a bit eccentric, and well, not someone I'd give a second thought to in *that* way. But this case has forced me to see a new side of her—like Rennie at my club in leotards, Rennie in my apartment gyrating in snug jeans and Rennie at a business banquet in an evening gown...and let me tell you, I like what I see very much. The forever kind of very much...if I can keep her from risking too much for me.

MEN at WORK

✈—MILLIONAIRE'S CLUB   🍎—BOARDROOM BOYS   ﾞ:—MAGNIFICENT MEN

ᗡ—TALL, DARK & SMART   💼—DOCTOR, DOCTOR   👢—MEN OF THE WEST

ﾊ门リ—MEN OF STEEL   §—MEN IN UNIFORM

MEN at WORK

HELEN R. MYERS

CONFIDENTIALLY YOURS

BOARDROOM BOYS

Silhouette Books

Published by Silhouette Books
America's Publisher of Contemporary Romance

SILHOUETTE BOOKS
300 East 42nd St.,
New York, N.Y. 10017

ISBN 0-373-81018-0

CONFIDENTIALLY YOURS

Printed in U.S.A.

Dear Reader,

Remember those great vintage *Thin Man* movies featuring Nick and Nora Charles, and much later, the slick and sexy "Moonlighting" series? Well, they all had something in common—men of intellect, men of purpose—and men smart enough to turn to a sharp lady when the chips were down.

I always thought attorney Nate Montgomery would have made an admirable grandson for Nick Charles. The first thing Nick would have done is to teach him the proper method of mixing a martini. And never-met-a-stranger Nora Charles would have had lunch regularly with equally enterprising private investigator Rennie Paris. But do you know what the predominant topic of conversation would have been? Not whodunit. Those guys!

MEN AT WORK are those special men who draw our attention from 9-to-5 drudgery to fantasizing about "what if...?" They can't help it. Ask Rennie. Once Nate got her to think like a woman instead of a PI her *undercover* days were numbered. Well...sort of.

Enjoy!

Helen R. Myers

Please address questions and book requests to:
Silhouette Reader Service
U.S.: 3010 Walden Ave., P.O. Box 1325, Buffalo, NY 14269
Canadian: P.O. Box 609, Fort Erie, Ont. L2A 5X3

Chapter One

"All right, Agnes, here are those letters I promised you," Nate Montgomery said, as he came out of his office and placed the stack of outgoing mail on her desk." Now if there's nothing else…" He paused and broke into a wide grin as she hastily hid her makeup compact under her desk. "Too late. I caught you."

"I was only trying to get something out of my eye."

"Fibber. You were looking at your hair again."

The middle-aged woman gave up trying to deceive him and drew out the compact once more. "Do you really think this frost job looks okay?" she asked, critically eyeing her reflection in the mirror. "I keep getting a feeling everyone is staring at me—even people I've never met before."

"Well, of course, they're staring, Agnes. You're a knockout. If I didn't know Wednesday was your night out with Harvey, I'd be tempted to make a pass at you myself."

"Oh, go on now." She patted her new coiffure and shot him a sly look from beneath her pale brown eyelashes. "If I thought you meant it, I'd tell Harvey to go play bingo without me."

"You're bad, Agnes."

"And I'm too old to change." She gave him an affectionate smile. "You're seriously leaving for the day?"

"Sshh." He held a finger up to his lips. Amusement twinkled in his dark eyes. "Don't let it get around, but I have it on good authority that there's a little Indian summer left outside and I want to soak up all I can before it heads south for the winter along with the geese."

"I don't blame you. Go. Enjoy—only don't forget your nine-o'clock tomorrow."

"Nine. Got it. Win a bundle tonight."

With a parting wave, he cut across the hallway and hurried through the double oak doors that all the attorneys at Dillard, Collins, Montgomery and Associates used for a quick escape instead of the official front entrance. After punching the down button at the elevators, he checked his watch and sighed with satisfaction.

Not only would he miss Chicago's rush-hour traffic, but he could still enjoy the sun from the balcony of his Lakeshore Drive condominium while grilling a steak on his indoor range. Maybe he would even finish that mystery novel he'd become engrossed in, before turning to the work in his briefcase.

No, first the briefs and then pleasure, he told himself as the elevator softly chimed its arrival and satin-finished steel doors whispered open. But he would placate himself with a glass of that vintage port he'd happened upon on a few months ago while shopping to restock his wine cabinet. He'd been waiting for the right weather, the right mood to open it; and there was something about that potation and September that was—consoling.

As he stepped in, he pressed the button to the first floor of the parking garage then leaned against the smooth back railing of the car for the ride down. A smile tugged at his lips because his mood was reminiscent of a kid playing hooky. But he wasn't a kid, he was thirty-eight; and it was more common for him to be one of the last to leave the office than the first. Why not? After all, it wasn't as if there was someone at home waiting for him, he thought, feeling the mildest twinge of regret, and he *did* enjoy his work.

But when he'd been at lunch, negotiating with Baker for a settlement on the DeWitt case, his attention had continuously wandered out the window of the restaurant, to the row of maple trees lining the sidewalk. Every gust of wind had tugged at the vibrantly colored leaves sending many dancing *en pointe* through the air in an amber-hued ballet. It had left him feeling restless, and slightly melancholy. A season was passing and he wanted to take a few moments to enjoy it.

When the elevator doors slid open, he exited into the garage whose great concrete pillars and linking steel girders never failed to spark the imaginative thought that he was inside some great beast. A living beast, he amended wryly hearing the sounds of activity rising from floors below. Halfway down the aisle, he spotted a woman getting into her car. Another truant soul, he mused, reaching into the pocket of his navy suit pants for his keys. His Mercedes was only four spots away from the elevator—one of the few benefits he could think of for arriving early.

Even before he got the key in the door lock, he spotted the brown envelope on the driver's seat.

The whimsical smile on his face became a perplexed frown; a few of the hairs on the back of his neck lifted, causing an unpleasant tingling sensation, and he missed the keyhole, scratching the charcoal-gray sedan's finish. With a muttered oath, he perfected his aim and unlocked the door.

How? he wondered, how had anyone gotten in? The windows were completely rolled up; all the doors were locked. There was no way...but someone *had* managed to get into his car, because he knew he hadn't left that envelope there.

He opened the door and reached for it. It was thin and weighed little. An unaddressed envelope, he discerned, turning it over, and sealed only by the metal prongs in the back. He set his briefcase down and, straightening, glanced around.

He was alone. The woman he'd noticed before was driving up to the ticket booth on the far side of the garage. Hold on, he told himself. Think. It wasn't his birthday and it wasn't April Fools' Day. Halloween was still a month away.... Try as he might, he couldn't come up with a single reason for someone to play a prank on him. But he wished he could.

All right, he thought, annoyance replacing concern. Someone was obviously trying to make a point, and he might as well see what it was. He straightened the prongs on the envelope and, slipping the flap free, glanced inside. A chill raced down his spine.

Pictures and a note.

Blackmail.

He didn't even have to read, or look, before the thought formulated. The strange thing was, he had the strongest urge to laugh. *Blackmail?* Used as a device in a mystery novel was one thing, but this was ridiculous.

The note was the uninspired cutouts of magazine and newspaper letters glued to a yellow lined sheet of paper from a legal pad. The wording was concise: *Get out of Chicago or these go to the press.*

What? he thought, still refusing to take this seriously, no dramatic ''by sundown'' for effect? He lifted the note to inspect the first picture.

''Oh, damn.''

The second and third photos were even more explicit. The male and female participants were clearly recognizable as himself and the wife of one of his current clients. This wasn't a prank.

Tight-lipped, he shoved the material back into the envelope, picked up his briefcase and slammed the car door. Usually conscientious, this time he didn't care if it was locked or not.

As he headed back toward the elevator, his heart was pounding, his pulse was racing—just as fast as it had been that first time he'd walked into a courtroom, fully comprehending what it meant to hold a person's fate in his hands. He could already feel his palms growing damp as he tightened his hold on the leather handle of his briefcase.

The ride up the elevator seemed to take twice as long as the ride down, but he tried to use it to his benefit—to slow his heartbeat and squelch the panicky feeling unsettling his stomach. It didn't escape him that he was experiencing the same feelings he knew his clients must have felt when they first came to his office, looking for answers, looking for a solution to their troubles. What was his standard opening line? *Try to relax.* Talk about vapid rhetoric. During the ride he vowed never to make such an inane remark again.

When he walked back through the double doors, he understood the surprised look on Agnes's face, but he didn't stop to explain. He just shook his head at her, indicating this wasn't the time to ask any questions, then went into his office and shut the door behind him.

There were those in the firm who said his office commanded the floor's best view of the surrounding city. As he dropped his briefcase onto an armchair, he ignored it. He also ignored everything else in the plush, yet comfortable office—except for the phone.

He rounded his desk and grabbed it as he would a lifeline, punched out the seven digits he'd memorized a long time ago and waited impatiently for the ringing to begin. After the second ring he heard the familiar voice of a woman he'd never met, but who was now his unwitting link to sanity.

"It's Montgomery," he said without preamble. "Tell her I need her. Now."

The nun drove the old Chevy into the parking lot of the car wash and pulled up behind the Lincoln Continental that was second in line for service. After shifting into park, she switched the ignition key to Off and the car shook, coughed and sputtered to an undignified death.

Unperturbed, she got out and beamed through her wire-framed glasses at the lanky young man walking toward her. "Give it the works, dear."

"Geez, Sister, it needs a paint job, not a wash'n wax," he muttered, eyeing the coupe that had more base coat showing than olive green.

"Do the best you can. I have to pick up the monsignor at the airport in an hour." She slipped a five-dollar bill into his hand. "Get me in behind that Mercedes and there's another one of these in it for you when I leave. The monsignor doesn't like to be kept waiting."

"Yes, *ma'am*."

As she walked across the wet asphalt, the persistent wind blowing off Lake Michigan pulled at her black habit and veil. She ducked her head against the cooling breeze and slipped the strap of her plain black purse over her shoulder before hurrying toward the door with the sign identifying the customer waiting lounge.

There were several people inside. One was sitting in a chrome-and-vinyl chair, sipping a cup of the complimentary coffee and browsing through the stack of magazines on the glass-and-chrome table. Another man and boy were eyeing the vending machines, though both looked as though they could afford to miss a few meals. The rest of the patrons stood along the line of windows that ran the length of the car conveyor, watching their vehicles' progress.

She dismissed them to concentrate on the hunk nearby who was checking his watch. An impatient hunk, she thought, clasping her hands sedately before her, but a hunk nevertheless.

Her heart made the crazy little leap it always did whenever she spotted him. Not smart, she would grant herself that, but reflexive and understandable. From his black hair to his Italian loafer-shod feet, he was every inch a prize specimen of masculinity. Her idea of a fantasy man if—oh, all right, she allowed, *when* she let herself visualize one: broad shouldered, lean but with the right amount of muscle tone, and a face that perfectly combined intelligence and virility. One look from those intense, deep-set eyes was enough to make a woman's pulse accelerate, and whenever he smiled…

Down, girl, she warned herself. *That's not for you, remember?* And even if he were, this was neither the time nor place. But a slight smile tugged the corner of her mouth upward, as she wondered how far his mouth would drop if he knew what she was thinking.

"You can stop checking your watch," she said, stepping up beside him. "I'm here. But this had better be good."

At the sound of that soothing yet amused voice, he turned, his eyes widening with surprise as he took in her attire. But then he asked himself, why should he be surprised? Wasn't he beyond the point of indulging in preconceived notions about how she would look when she arrived for one of their meetings? After two years, he'd come to realize that there were only two givens when he thought of Rennie Paris; one was that she was the most reliable private investigator he'd ever hired, and the other was that she was the most eccentric.

"Called you away from something interesting, did I?" he drawled, relaxing his compressed lips into a reluctant smile.

"I was at St. Paul's. They have some nut over there who thinks he's Michelangelo. He's putting his rendition of the Sistine Chapel on the backs of the church pews. If you ask me, he smacks more of a mad Dali."

"I thought perhaps this was your way of doing penance for overcharging me on the Nelligan case."

A young mother walked by with her baby. Rennie nodded, her smile serene. But under her breath she muttered, "Come on, Montgomery. After almost catching pneumonia, standing out in the rain waiting for Nelligan's two-timing partner to show up with those prints he was selling to their competition? I figure I earned that fee."

"With what you charged me, you could have paid for a trip to the Caribbean *and* taken a private nurse along with you."

"Ooh, a six-foot-tall one with great biceps, I hope?"

"Whatever," he replied, refusing to be baited. "What are you driving?"

She indicated the green Chevy following his onto the conveyor. Nate winced.

"God, Rennie. Couldn't you borrow something?"

"That *is* borrowed."

Nate suffered a second glance. "You mean there are two wrecks like yours out on the streets?"

"Be nice. Anyway, mine's back in the shop making strange noises again."

"Ever think it's trying to tell you something?"

Nate shook his head knowing it would be a waste of time to try to convince her that it was more economical to buy a new car. Instead he eyed her outfit again, his gaze lingering momentarily on the support hose and orthopedic shoes that hid what he'd too rarely identified as a luscious pair of legs. Why she insisted on downplaying any attractive feature she might have was something he'd never resolved to any degree of satisfaction.

"I suppose I should be grateful you weren't

helping one of your street friends, or you would have come dressed like a bag lady.''

Rennie told herself that it was ridiculous to feel the tiny hurt that stabbed her heart, but it took effort to lift her chin and with quiet dignity reply, ''The point is that you called and I'm here.''

He closed his eyes briefly. Then, following an inexplicable impulse, he leaned over and gave her a light kiss on the cheek. ''I'm sorry. That was uncalled for. It's just that sometimes I'd prefer to meet in a more businesslike way.''

''Whose business? Anyway, you know the rules, Nate.''

Rules. Right, he thought, glancing away with frustration. After two years he could recite them in his sleep. Contact only through an answering service, payment through a post-office box, meetings where he swore she *worked* on looking plain, or worse yet, arrived wearing any manner of disguise—depending on the case she'd been working on when he called. He was grateful for the day he'd inherited her phone number from a retiring attorney, but there were times, like now when *his* neck was in the noose, that he wondered if he would do well to remember that she wasn't the only private investigator in town.

''It's a bad one this time, isn't it?'' she asked softly, still feeling the touch of his lips. She barely resisted lifting a hand to her cheek. "A new client?"

"No. Me." Nate glanced down at the envelope in his hands and began to hand it to her. But just as she took hold of it, he tightened his grip. "Rennie...at the risk of sounding redundant, this *is* in the strictest confidence, agreed?"

She lifted a tawny eyebrow. "When have I ever let you down?"

He didn't miss hearing the slight chill that entered her voice, a voice that on the phone was often teasing and mellifluous. The same chill was reflected in her eyes, and yet even her ugly glasses couldn't hide that they were her best feature—slightly almond shaped, the color reminding him of jewels, more specifically emeralds.

"It seems to be my day for being tactless." He released his hold and after unbuttoning the jacket of his three-piece suit, slid his hands into his pants pockets. At least he didn't have to worry about offending her with the contents, he thought, turning back to watch his car pass from the soaping area to the rinse section. If he was certain of one thing, it was that Rennie wasn't easily shocked. She'd shared enough stories about her experiences with him to know that there wasn't much she hadn't seen.

But he wasn't exactly prepared to hear her smother a low laugh, either.

"It's *not* me," he growled.

She'd known that the moment she'd taken a second, closer look at the male subject's shoulders and hips and noticed something wasn't quite in sync with that of the man she felt she knew. Relief left her feeling almost cheerful.

"What a shame. I've always wondered what you'd look like without your tie." Because she was rereading the attached note, she missed seeing his smoldering glare. "My, my...you *do* have a problem here, don't you? Who's the lady?—and I use the term loosely."

"Karyn Jerome, the wife of Philip Jerome, a client," Nate muttered, closing his hands into fists. "I'm handling his suit against the Morgan Towers complex up by Washington Park."

Rennie pursed her lips together and whistled silently. "I've read about that in the papers. He was supposed to be the architect for phase two of the Towers, but he was fired."

"For flimsy reasons and *without* being paid the agreed fee for breach of contract."

"I suppose you're aware who's allegedly behind the Morgan group?"

"I am. And I also know they're not thrilled with Mr. Jerome's decision to take them to court. The question is, are you willing to find out if they're responsible for this? I wouldn't blame you if you said no," he added gruffly. As good as Rennie was, Nate couldn't imagine her wanting to risk running afoul of the mob.

Rennie considered his words, her heart in turmoil with her mind. There were times when, after Stan Freeman retired from practicing law, she'd regretted allowing him to pass on her phone number to Nate. From the beginning she'd recognized that Nate was too handsome, too smooth, too sexy even for *her* to remain indifferent to him. Yet he was also a reminder of all that had gone wrong in her life, and of dreams that she'd closed off her heart to.

But hearing the concern in his voice, seeing it reflected in his eyes, made her decide that this was a moment to cherish, not regret. The pleasure she felt from realizing he cared—if only a little— was worth risking a bit of heartache.

"Nonsense," she replied with a bright smile. "How can I tell my favorite client no? Anyway, you don't *really* think they'd drop a harmless thing like me in cement, do you?"

"Jokes aside, be careful, Rennie. If anything happened to you I'd—miss you." He watched the teasing light go out of her eyes and something tender take its place. Inside he felt as if his heart hit its brakes and came to a brief but total halt. It didn't, of course, but that's what it felt like. Crazy.

"Well." She tore her gaze from his and nervously glanced around. Lord, what was the matter with her? "I suppose I'll just have to be careful that that doesn't happen, won't I?"

"Find out what or rather *who's* behind this and I'll buy you that plane ticket to the Caribbean myself."

"That's what I like about you, Nate. You have such a keen appreciation for services rendered. I'll be in touch." She slipped the envelope into her purse and patted his hand. "Be a dear and take care of my bill for me, will you? The only cash I'm carrying is tucked in the holster of my .380 and I don't think Father Carmichael could take the stress of hearing that not only did one of his nuns lift her skirts in public, but that she carries an automatic strapped to her thigh as well."

Nate burst into laughter and, shaking his head, reached for his billfold. "Rennie, sometimes I think if I deal with you much longer, I'll wind up as crazy as you are."

"Yeah, but what a way to go," she drawled, wiggling her eyebrows at him. "Oh! And can you spare an extra five?"

He barely had a chance to reply before she plucked it out of his wallet herself. "What's that for?"

"Contingencies, dear heart."

Nate watched her walk away, feeling as drained and confused as if he'd just been dropped from a tornado that had landed him in another time zone. But even so, despite everything, he had to admit she'd succeeded in making him feel better. She *always* made him feel better. A little rattled, slightly frustrated, but better.

"Who are you, Rennie Paris?" he wondered aloud, and not for the first time. Would the day ever come when she would let him really get to know her the way he would like to? He hoped so. He had a feeling she was a pretty special person beneath all the hype and mystery. Yet he knew the decision was hers to make. So he waited, and wondered.

But right now, he reminded himself, he had a more serious question to ponder—like how was she going to find out who was behind this mess? And what was he going to do once she did?

"One thing at a time," he sighed. Rubbing the remaining tenseness out of the back of his neck muscles, he went to pay both their bills.

Chapter Two

Rennie returned to the west side of the city and St. Paul's, where she checked in with Father Carmichael before deciding to call it a day. After changing back into her own cropped denim jacket, T-shirt and pleated twill trousers, she drove over to her neighborhood garage and returned the Chevy to Charlie Sanchez.

Charlie greeted her with a mournful look and the news that her car wasn't ready yet. She hadn't expected to hear otherwise. Nate was right about her clunker. But how could she tell him her refusal to let go was based on an emotional need to make things last in a world where she'd been proven to be one of the throwaways? So she negotiated a new deal with Charlie and left, satisfied knowing she could borrow his car again tomorrow. It had the better radio anyway, she thought, heading for home.

While waiting for a light change at the corner, delicious aromas drifted over from Giammarco's market. She decided to give in to temptation and crossed over for a fresh loaf of Italian bread, before walking the rest of the way to her apartment.

She lived on the fringes of Little Italy and the detours, combined with the three-block trip home, took her nearly an hour. The good weather had lured many of her neighbors out to their front stoops, the children to the sidewalks and streets, and everyone seemed to be in the mood to chat.

The West Side was a mélange of ethnic neighborhoods, its roots going back to the nineteenth and early twentieth centuries. Rennie had been calling it home for the last eighteen of her thirty years, living in the same attic apartment she'd once shared with her friend, mentor and foster parent Fred Paris.

By the time she reached her building and climbed the four floors to her small apartment, it was six o'clock. As she put her key in the deadbolt lock, she could hear the news begin on the TV she'd left playing inside. She also heard a wail, warning her that she was going to have some explaining to do.

"I know, Arabella, I know," she crooned, easing inside and locking the door behind her. She turned to the gray Persian cat perched on the armrest of her sofa and winced at the final howl she gave her. "All right! So I couldn't take you out for an afternoon stroll. Give me a break. *Somebody* has to earn the rent money around here, you know."

The cat turned her head away to watch the news anchorman on TV. Rennie knew what that meant and narrowed her eyes in the same way her pet had initially glared at her.

"Ha! You think I'm impressed? Let me tell you what's inside this bag, Arabella. Fresh scallops. Seven ninety-nine a pound and Mr. Giammarco *swears* they just came in. Either I get some respect around here or these scallops become quiche."

Arabella let Rennie get all the way to the kitchen before following. Finally she rubbed against her mistress's leg. As intended, the movement drew a smile from Rennie.

"I should have named you Delilah," she muttered, glancing up as the news anchorman announced the lead story. "What do you think of him, Belle? Is he better than the other two? Maybe we should become feminists and boycott all three until they put on a female anchor."

The cat ignored the comment, hopped up on a bar stool and scratched the shopping bag. Rennie nodded.

"That makes two of us; I don't make my best decisions on an empty stomach, either. Here, then," she said, taking out the shellfish wrapped in white deli paper.

Rennie reached over to the dish drainer for her pet's saucer, a lovely piece of china with gold-leaf trim she'd found at a pattern discontinuation sale. As she emptied the scallops onto the dish, Arabella stood on her hind legs, bracing her front paws on the white laminated countertop.

"How many times have I told you? No paws on the counter. And I want you to remember you're a lady and not a hog," she added, placing the meal before her.

Rennie tossed the paper into the garbage and washed her hands. While the charismatic news-caster on TV described the latest drug bust and identified another state official under indictment by the grand jury, she took out a jug of wine from the refrigerator and poured herself a glass of Chablis. Then she tossed two hot dogs into her microwave.

"Everybody's got problems. You should hear what happened to Nate." She sighed and took a sip of her wine. "Mmm. But first let me get these pins out of my hair. They're already beginning to give me a headache. Stay out of my glass," she warned her pet as she hurried for the bath-room.

She returned minutes later, her hair cascading down her back in a thick mass of freshly brushed honey-blond curls. After replacing the news broadcast with stereo music, she retrieved her hot dogs, plus a jar of mustard out of the refrigerator, and took a seat on the bar stool beside Arabella's. While a current top-twenty favorite played in the background, she took a bite of hot dog and fresh bread, gloomily eyeing the envelope sticking out of her purse.

"You know what's in there?" she asked the cat, who'd devoured her dinner and was preoccupied with washing her paws. "Never mind. You're not the worldly-wise creature you think you are. Just take it from me, things don't bode well for Nate."

At the sound of his name, Arabella lifted her head and gave Rennie a soft mew. Rennie rolled her eyes.

"Yes, *our* Nate. How many do we know? You were so busy stuffing your face you didn't hear me the first time, did you? Somebody's blackmailing him. They want him out of Chicago."

Apparently that was too much for Arabella. She jumped off her stool and went to her favorite perch on the living-room windowsill to gaze trancelike outside.

"Yeah, I know exactly how you feel," Rennie muttered. She turned back to her dinner and decided that whatever appetite she'd had was gone. She dropped the hot dog back onto her plate and reached for her wineglass. "Darn you anyway,

Nate Montgomery. Why did you have to get yourself into this mess?''

There were clients she'd had much longer, but she hadn't been joking when she called him her favorite—though it was fine for him to think she *was* only teasing. Contrary to popular belief, she wasn't a glutton for punishment; there was no need for him to discover how true it was.

It wasn't simply a matter of his being the most attractive man she'd ever met, or that she truly believed he was a terrific attorney, and a generous employer—despite his inclination to grumble about her fees. Over the past two years, she'd had an opportunity to see him under some pretty adverse conditions, yet she'd come to care for him as a person—more, as a man.

It wasn't supposed to have happened, and it was, of course, a hopeless situation. Even if she was his type—and there was no doubt in her mind that she wasn't—she'd learned a long time ago that she wasn't meant for lasting relationships. Caring was also dangerous; in her line of work it was healthier to keep a clear head and concentrate on business.

But there it was, and there didn't seem to be anything she could do about it, short of telling him that she wanted to end their business relationship. Lately that was more and more of a temptation, but he would only demand an explanation, and she hadn't yet been able to come up with one she thought he would accept. So she was caught in a self-imposed deadlock where she took one day, one case at a time; and each time they met she worried about how much more difficult it was becoming to hide her feelings for him.

Now something else she'd been dreading had happened: the noble eagle had become prey. Nate had upset someone enough that they wanted him out of Chicago. But who, and why? He was certain it was the Morgan Towers group. Morgan Towers…he couldn't know it, but that made things both easier and more difficult for her.

She knew the man who owned the complex. Once she'd done Mario DePalma a service. She'd been working on a case and he had benefited from the results.

Afterward he'd been most grateful. He'd vowed that if she ever needed anything, she had only to tell him and it would be hers. Of course, she'd also made herself a promise never to allow herself to get into the kind of predicament where he could be of service in return.

She hadn't, had she? But now there was this thing with Nate and, as she was only beginning to realize, there wasn't much she wouldn't do for him.

The only question that remained was, would Mario DePalma keep his word? She certainly hoped so, she thought, rising to refill her glass, because first thing tomorrow, she was going to find out.

At ten the following morning, Rennie walked into the lobby of the Morgan Hotel and headed straight for the Executive Registration desk. She wore a pale turquoise, soft jersey jumpsuit with a matching hood and dyed-to-match suede boots. The casual but chic look earned her admiring glances from men and a few appraising looks from women. However, she noticed neither from behind her stylishly large sunglasses; she was too busy camouflaging a last-minute attack of nerves.

The receptionist at the desk eyed her coolly. "Can I help you?"

Such enthusiasm, Rennie thought, keeping her hands in her pockets and her expression equally cool. "Mr. DePalma, please."

"Do you have an appointment?"

"I wasn't aware old acquaintances needed one."

"I'm sorry. Mr. DePalma doesn't see *anyone* without an appointment."

"Tell him it's Rennie. I think he'll change his mind."

Less than five minutes later a square-bodied, expensively suited man stepped from the service elevator. Rennie wondered fleetingly whether anyone *ever* mistook him for an executive.

"C'mon over here," he mumbled, jerking his

head toward a more quiet corner of the lobby. Once behind an antique armoire, he glared at her resentfully. "You carrying?"

Rennie turned her pockets inside out, indicating all she had with her were her keys. After a few seconds, she adjusted her clothing.

"I still gotta frisk you," the broad-shouldered bodyguard told her.

Rennie slid her sunglasses half an inch down her nose and gave him a mild look over the rim. "Rocco, you lay a finger on the merchandise and I'm going to have to do what I did the last time you tried that. You don't want to embarrass yourself in front of Mr. DePalma's hotel guests, do you?"

The veins in his neck bulged and his face turned crimson. With a murderous look, he spun around and indicated she should follow him to the elevator.

They rode up in silence. That neither surprised nor disappointed Rennie. She'd learned during the occasion of their initial introduction that Rocco wasn't the world's most entertaining conversationalist.

When they reached the penthouse, the elevator doors slid open to reveal two other men, silent sentinels standing in the marble-floored foyer. Despite the fact that there had been a camera in the elevator, it was clear that DePalma believed in the value of auxiliary precautions.

"Rennie!"

Out on the terrace an elderly man waved from his breakfast table. Rennie curved her lips into a wry smile and crossed the white-carpeted living room, then passed through the opened sliding glass doors to join him.

The penthouse overlooked Washington Park and to the south, across the river, Rennie could see the part of downtown known as the Loop, where the Sears Tower stood out among the other highrises glistening in the bright morning sun. Behind Mario DePalma was the John Hancock Building and beyond it Lake Michigan. He'd come far from the West Side neighborhood where he'd grown up. Rennie couldn't fault his obvious pride in his accomplishments, but she had her reservations on how he'd achieved most of them.

As he gestured to the seat opposite him, she removed her sunglasses. The small courtesy earned her an even warmer smile.

"It's been too long. You look splendid."

"You know me; any chance to dress up," she replied, taking the proffered seat.

The wiry-built man chuckled in appreciation of the shared joke, while he adjusted the linen napkin on his lap. "Ah, Rennie. You know I've missed you. When are you going to come work for me?"

"Right after the pope beatifies Rocco."

"You're too much. Please—" He indicated the dish-laden cart and the attendant standing beside it. "Join me for some breakfast."

"No, thanks. But don't let me stop you."

"At least some coffee. This breeze has a bite. It'll warm you."

"All right, coffee, then." She glanced at the young man waiting. "Black, please."

Mario DePalma clucked like a mother hen as he picked up his own cup. "You should take a little cream, a little sugar; putting on a few pounds wouldn't hurt you."

"They might if they slowed me down." As the waiter placed the cup before her, she murmured her thanks.

"Always the professional. How's business?"

"I can't complain. Yours?"

His mouth twitched. He finished his coffee and motioned for a refill. "Couldn't be better. But you aren't here to exchange pleasantries, are you?"

"I'm afraid not." For a moment Rennie hesitated, hoping she wasn't being presumptuous. "A few years ago you told me you owed me a favor," she began.

"You saved my grandson's life. It's not a thing I'm likely to forget."

"How is the boy?"

"In his second year of college and complaining about the amount of studying he has to do.

How quickly the young forget, eh?'' He pushed his plate away. ''So…finally you have a need to collect. I'm honored.''

Rennie sipped her coffee and lifted both eyebrows in a gesture of skepticism. ''You might not think so when I tell you what it is.''

He leaned back in his chair and signaled the waiter to remove his plate. When the man had retreated into the penthouse and they were alone, he glanced out over the city and sighed.

''You're not pleased that you had to come to me.''

''I like you, Mr. DePalma. But I can't say I approve of your—business affiliations.''

''I appreciate your candor. Now tell me what it is that's taken the sparkle out of those lovely green eyes.''

Rennie pushed her cup away and folded her arms on the glass-topped table. ''I have a client who's being asked to leave Chicago.''

''And he doesn't want to relocate?''

''He was born here and he has an established business.''

''But the party inviting him to leave is unsympathetic.''

''To the point of resorting to blackmail. Photographs, Mr. DePalma. Tampered photographs.''

''Effective, though tasteless.'' He gave her a

curious look. "Are you having difficulty locating the blackmailer?"

"My client seems to think he knows the individual responsible. You see, Mr. DePalma, the lady in the photographs is the wife of *his* client— Philip Jerome."

"Philip— Ah." Mario DePalma, having been startled out of his usual calm, sat back in his chair again and thoughtfully ran his fingers over his wide but thin mouth. He drew his silver eyebrows together, though his dark eyes reflected more confusion than concern. "I'd heard you've been doing work for Nate Montgomery. A fine attorney. But really, Rennie, does he actually believe that *I'm* responsible for this? Do you?"

She met his gaze unwaveringly. "I prefer to think that if there is a connection, the decision was made by someone who didn't come to you for approval."

Slightly mollified, he gave her a vague smile. "Fred Paris taught you well. I wish more young people would show such respect. But truly, Rennie," he gestured expansively, "I'm running a legitimate operation these days. Philip Jerome was under contract; I didn't like his work; I had him fired. *Finis.* The details I leave to the lawyers to handle."

Rennie toyed with the sunglasses she'd laid on the table. "I don't know whether to be relieved or disappointed."

"I understand. Now you know you must look for someone else, someone who thinks they're being clever in making me look guilty." His expression hardened. "You tell your Mr. Montgomery that his enemy is now my enemy."

Her Mr. Montgomery? The phrasing made Rennie uncomfortable. The last thing she needed was DePalma thinking this was more than business.

"He won't accept your help."

"Nevertheless it's available should he need it."

Rennie stood, knowing she was being dismissed. "I'll tell him. Thank you for seeing me."

"The pleasure was mine. And Rennie...the favor remains between us," he reminded her.

She smiled and started for the door. When he called her once again, she turned to see him raise a finger in warning. "You also tell Montgomery to watch his back. Only someone who's looking over your shoulder can read your playing hand."

She slipped on her sunglasses. "That's crossed my mind, too. Goodbye."

The older man watched her until the elevator doors closed behind her. "Not goodbye, Rennie," he murmured. "*Arrivederci*. Definitely later. Rocco!"

When he wasn't tied up in court or with other appointments, Nate often liked to go to his health club at noon instead of having lunch. But when Rennie called and they made arrangements to meet there, strengthening his cardiovascular system was the last thing on his mind.

He pulled into the club's parking lot, feeling the tension he'd been trying to ignore all morning mounting inside him. She'd refused to explain anything over the phone—but then that was standard procedure with her—leaving him to guess at the news she might have. It wasn't doing wonders for his nerves.

It was still early for the usual noon crowd, but as he entered the building and walked down the long corridors toward the changing rooms, he saw that the aerobics room and gym were already busy. Could Rennie be here yet? He'd asked her how she planned to get in when membership cards were required, and she'd told him not to worry about it. The important thing, she'd said, was for him to appear to hold to routine and give every appearance that things were normal.

Normal, he thought, entering the men's changing room and going straight to his locker. What a joke; he hadn't felt *normal* since he'd found that envelope in his car.

As he changed into a blue-and-green tank top and matching shorts, he wished she would at least have told him what she would be wearing. It struck him that he wasn't even sure what color hair Rennie had, because usually she had it tucked under a scarf, baseball cap or ski cap, depending on the weather. It wasn't dark, he thought remembering that her eyebrows were tawny—which meant what? Damn, was he *that* unobservant? He rubbed the back of his neck half wishing they'd made arrangements to meet at some quiet restaurant. He wasn't hungry, but he was beginning to feel as though he could use a drink.

"Hi, Nate. Going to play a few sets of tennis?"

He waved at one of the regulars passing by. "No, not enough time. Just going to burn off a little steam on the bikes, I think." Rennie said she would find him. But deciding it would be better if he placed himself somewhere easily accessible, he headed for the equipment room.

An elderly man was getting off one of the bikes as he approached, leaving only a middle-aged woman at the end of the row. Nate found himself eyeing her cautiously only to berate himself a moment later for being a fool. Granted, he'd often met Rennie in the midst of a case that required a masquerade like that nun's outfit yesterday, but even *she* couldn't pull off something like this. The woman would have to stretch to be five feet tall—and that left her a good six or seven inches under Rennie's height. *You're getting punchy,* he warned himself, shaking his head as he climbed on a bike to begin a comfortable cycling pace.

Several yards away from him were the rowing machines, where one plump woman was giving her all to finish her quota, but from the way she was gasping, Nate guessed it wouldn't be long before an instructor came over to tell her to take a break. However, when he glanced across the room, he saw that the nearest instructor was otherwise preoccupied. He was taking a slender blonde around, showing her the different equipment. A new member, he mused. Lucky instructor, though he could only appreciate a back view of the young woman in the aqua-and-white striped leotards.

Her hair was lovely, a bountiful fall of wild curls caught in a ponytail, yet still reaching well down her back. The color reminded him of something between honey and gold. He found himself wishing she would turn around so that he could see her face; already her thoroughbred long legs triggered a response in him that was all male appreciation. Lousy timing, he thought, dropping his gaze to check the gauges on his bike. If he didn't have this mess hanging over his head and if he didn't have to meet Rennie, he would have made a point of introducing himself to her. As it was—

"Nate? Nathanial Elliot Montgomery—it *is* you!"

At the sound of that familiar voice, he jerked his head up and stared in disbelief as the blonde, now only yards away, stood beaming at him. She even had Rennie's eyes, but how could it be? he wondered dazedly. This woman was striking!

Before he could think to react, she rushed over to him and threw her arms around his neck. "Play along with me," she whispered into his ear. "I'll explain later."

"Rennie?"

"Isn't he wonderful? He actually remembers my name," she said to the bewildered and slightly disappointed instructor. "Yes, it's me, you darling man. Rennie Paris. I haven't seen you since—when? Allison and Bill's wedding, wasn't it?"

"Bob," he corrected, then thought, *Wait a minute...how did she know that?*

"Whatever. You know I've never been good with names." Ignoring the way his eyebrow shot up at that, she eased his fingers from their firm grip on her waist—at least enough to turn to the muscle-bound instructor. "Darrell, would you mind terribly if I just used this bike beside Nate so we can catch up on old times?"

"But, Rennie, I haven't finished showing you the rest of the facilities."

"And I'm anxious to see them. But you've already spent so much time with me, and I feel I'm depriving the other members of your knowledge and assistance. Why, right over there is a lady who I'm sure could use a little attention," she said, indicating the now purple-faced woman on the rowing machine.

"Holy—Mrs. Kleinman? Delores! Land-ho, Delores!"

As he hurried off to her, Rennie smothered a laugh and turned back to Nate, only to find he'd missed the whole scene because he was still staring at her as though she'd descended from a flying saucer. No, not quite in that way, she amended—unless he had a thing for lady martians.

She cleared her throat and once again tried to remove his hands from her waist. "I think the coast is clear."

"My God, I don't believe it."

"Will you let go?"

"You're even wearing mascara and—*lipstick.*"

"Lots of women do," she replied, managing to make it sound droll though her heart was beginning to pound.

"Not you. It seems you've made a career out of downplaying your femininity." Nate dropped his gaze from the curls slipping free from her ponytail to her jogging shoes and shook his head with disbelief. "Seeing you like this, I can't help but wonder why?"

"Yeah? Well, keep wondering because this is neither the time nor the place to explain."

Nate sensed her rising agitation, but even more, he sensed a nervousness in her. His bemused smile turned into a grin. There was something about seeing Rennie Paris on the defensive that was oddly satisfying. He decided to savor the moment a little longer. "I thought you were supposed to be glad to see me?" he drawled.

"I already gave you a hug. What do you want?"

"Old friends exchange kisses."

She narrowed her eyes in warning but leaned forward to give him a quick peck on the cheek. "There—satisfied?"

"Hardly."

Before she could react, he pulled her against him and closed his mouth over hers. Shock buffeted through Rennie in waves, causing her to sway. She put her hands on his chest to regain her balance, and curled her fingers into the soft material of his shirt as she reacted to the firm pressure of his lips. Oh, God, she thought. She hadn't wanted to find out it felt even better than she'd imagined.

Even before she could collect her senses and think to push him away, he ended the kiss and helped her regain her footing. He was smiling again, but there was also a hint of tension around his mouth.

"That's for trying to play me for a fool all this time."

"*What?* I did no such thing!"

He glanced over her shoulder and noticed a few people were still watching them. Reluctantly he released her. "We'll discuss it later."

Don't hold your breath, Rennie thought, backing into the bike beside him. She recovered her balance and spent the next few moments concentrating on familiarizing herself with it, but more importantly regrouping her scattered emotions.

Control, she told herself. She had to regain control of the situation and keep her personal feelings out of this. She also had to keep Nate from getting any ideas, she added, remembering the annoyance and determination she'd seen flash in his dark eyes. That was really the problem. She'd expected him to be somewhat surprised when he saw her, but she hadn't anticipated this kind of reaction.

Nate tried to keep his gaze from straying to her, but failed. Talk about makeovers, he thought. How could he not have noticed her potential before? Flawless skin, a heart-shaped face, exotic almond-shaped eyes in a shade of green that had always captured his imagination...she was a delight—and he wanted to strangle her.

"Why now?" he asked, posing the question that was in the forefront of his mind.

"Suffice it to say I have my reasons." She

thought about her plan and told herself she must have been out of her mind to even consider it.

Nate caught her biting her lower lip, remembering the satiny smooth texture of it and had to force himself to focus on business. "You don't have good news for me, do you?"

"Depends on how you look at it. The point is DePalma didn't send you that envelope."

Nothing else could have cleared his head more quickly. "Are you sure?"

Rennie expelled her breath in a long hiss. "Great. Now that you know I'm a blonde, you're going to start questioning everything I say? Yes, I'm sure. I asked him myself this morning."

"You went to see *DePalma*?"

"Keep this up, counselor, and we're going to be on these bikes all afternoon."

"How do you know him?" he asked, clarifying himself.

"It's a long story, and, for your information, none of your business. All that should matter to you is that he said he was more than willing to let his lawyers work out the Jerome problem with you. I believe him, Nate."

His answering look was grim. "But what about those photos? They're incriminating evidence he can't easily dismiss."

"I know it, and he's not thrilled with the idea of someone using him as a scapegoat, either." She paused as someone walked by. "He gave me a message for you. He said to tell you that your enemy was now his enemy and that he would welcome the opportunity to help you, if—"

"Hold it right there."

"I told him there was no way you would accept."

"Good." Nate relaxed, but only for a moment because he quickly realized what Rennie had meant before; he was now in more trouble than ever. If DePalma wasn't behind this, it left the field of suspects wide open and he didn't know where to begin looking.

"I made a few phone calls before I came here," Rennie said, resisting the urge to reach out to him in a gesture of reassurance. "I had an idea that I might be able to at least find a source for whoever did the artwork on the photos. But so far I'm drawing a blank."

"Where does that leave us?"

"You try to relax and I keep looking."

He was already tired of feeling helpless. "I don't have any other leads to give you."

"Maybe the next contact from our blackmailer will give us the break we need."

"How can you be sure he'll make contact again?"

"Well, you haven't packed your bags, have you? He only has one other option—other than to follow through with his threat."

Nate swore softly. "I don't even want to think about that."

"I didn't say I thought he *would* follow through. It depends on his motive."

"Explain."

"DePalma said something that confirmed my own impressions. He said you should watch your back because whoever was behind this was someone close." She met his intent look. "That would suggest they'd have to have some pretty strong feelings to want to go through all this trouble. Our challenge is to figure out what those feelings are. Revenge? Jealousy?"

Nate stopped pedaling, a queasy feeling rising in his stomach. It made sense, but the idea wasn't a pleasant one because either way, the black-mailer had to despise him. He didn't want to think it could be someone he might consider a friend.

Rennie could see the worry on his face and felt compassion seep through the barriers of her resolve. "Hey, lighten up, counselor. We're not going to convince anyone that we're having a happy reunion with that expression," she said, trying to coax him into a better mood.

He shot her an apologetic look and began pedaling again. "I suppose all we can do now is sit and wait."

"Well..."

"You have an idea?"

She did have a suggestion to offer him when she'd first arrived. At that point the idea had seemed foolproof; but now that it was time to tell him, she'd lost her nerve. Foolproof? Foolish was more like it. It would never work. She could never pull it off.

"Rennie, talk to me."

"Well, the logical thing to do is to prepare ourselves for the next move," she began hesitantly.

"Granted, but how?"

Rennie drew a deep breath, then shaking her head, expelled it. "No, I can't. Forget it. It's a bad idea."

"Rennie, *how*?"

Get it over with quickly, she told herself, and then pray that he doesn't laugh too loudly. "Oh, blast it all... How do you feel about having an affair?"

Chapter Three

He didn't laugh. What he *did* do was insist they leave the club and go someplace where they could talk freely. Rennie agreed making little comment, deciding it would be the lesser evil to be humiliated with a select audience.

After they changed, and he phoned his office, they drove to a quiet North Side restaurant. The maître d' greeted them with a warmth that told Rennie they were in one of Nate's favorite haunts. When he showed them to a secluded corner table in the romantically dark dining room, she was sure of it.

She took an abnormally deep interest in the brocade wallpaper, the white table linen, the menu and then the red rose in the middle of the table. Anything to avoid looking at Nate, who was having no problem deciding that for the moment, *she* was what interested him the most.

A cocktail waitress came by to take their drink order. Normally Rennie didn't touch anything alcoholic until she was home and finished work for the day, but deciding her nerves needed it, she ordered herself a glass of white wine. Nate ordered a bourbon and water. Both of them hesitated when the waiter stepped forward to take their lunch orders. Rennie chose the first thing her gaze fell to on the menu, even though she wasn't particularly fond of spinach salads.

Nate was even worse; he ordered a steak with all the trimmings, then wondered how he was going to force himself to eat any of it.

"Now," he said, when they were finally alone. "Would you care to repeat that little remark you made a while ago?"

"Not really."

"Humor me anyway."

"There's no need to rub it in."

Nate felt guilty because he sensed Rennie was still very nervous. In a courtroom, he followed the theory that all was fair, but in private—particularly with women—he was far more respectful of a person's sensitivity. Yet she'd rattled him profoundly in the past hour and, to his way of thinking, it was about time she had a taste of her own medicine.

"Look at things from my perspective," he said

dryly. "A beautiful woman has propositioned me. I only want to make sure I'm not misinterpreting anything."

"I'm not— You *know* I only meant that we should pretend."

Nate frowned, trying to figure out what she'd first begun to say. Then it came to him. She really *didn't* believe she was attractive. Could it be that she'd downplayed her looks for so long that she'd grown blind to what she saw in the mirror? Possibly, he thought, taking in the picture she made dressed in her jumpsuit, her hair a virtual halo of curls. Incredibly blind.

"Rennie," he murmured more gently, "what do you say if we start over again?"

Her gaze dropped to her clasped hands in her lap. *Pull yourself together,* she scolded herself. She was supposed to be a professional; this was business....

"All right." She swallowed to ease the dryness of her throat. "This is what I came up with. DePalma was right—whoever's pulling this stunt is someone you know, someone you see frequently, either on a social or business basis. Now you have one of two options. You can either call the police in the hopes that it will scare off the blackmailer, or you can give him a false sense of security by using me covertly."

Nate nodded slowly. "I get it. If we pretend

we're—involved, it will validate your spending so much time around me.''

''Exactly. I thought about being your long lost cousin or something, but I decided no one would buy you dragging a relative around with you wherever you went.'' Warming to her subject, Rennie leaned toward him, unaware of the excitement that lit her eyes. ''I would have the opportunity to study the people around you without them knowing they're even suspects.''

Nate considered that for a moment before nodding. ''I like that idea much better than calling in the police. I'd have to show them the pictures, yet the more people who see them, the more chance there'd be of a leak to the press. Neither Karyn nor I need that kind of publicity.''

The cocktail waitress returned with their drinks. When she was gone, Nate lifted his glass and touched it to Rennie's. ''It's a good idea— and don't think I'm not aware of what you're offering to do for me.''

''Well, we're not exactly talking about hardship duty here.''

It took her a moment to realize what that sounded like and, when she did, a rush of heat flooded her cheeks. Nate's low, wicked laugh didn't help.

''Why, Rennie, you're blushing. I'll take that as a double compliment.''

She was sipping her wine and almost choked

on it. "What I meant was that appearances can go a long way."

"That's why you came on to me at the club as if we'd already been—er, fond of each other?"

"Exactly. Since I knew we'd need to work on an accelerated timetable that gave us a head start."

It most certainly did, Nate thought, remembering how appealing it had felt—once the shock had worn off—to have her arms around his neck, to kiss her. He found himself wanting to experience the moment again, and again. He smiled wryly at what was proving to be a very strange turn of events. "Let me ask you, how did you know about Allison and Bob?"

"Professional secret."

"You've been checking up on me, haven't you?" He wasn't exactly annoyed; after all, when Stan had given him her number, he'd asked a lot of questions, too. Not that it did him much good.

"As I told you a long time ago, when I take on a client it's not your average working relationship. If I'm going to risk my reputation, maybe even my health, I want to know the person is worth it."

"And am I?" he asked, holding her gaze with his own.

There it was again, Rennie thought. She'd felt it the moment when he'd first put his arms around her, an achy feeling that pulled from some point deep inside. But it was a feeling she knew she had to resist.

"I'm here, aren't I?"

Nate would have liked her to be more complimentary, but once again sensed her putting barriers between them. Why? he wondered, and how did he get her to stop? That kiss they'd shared had been all too brief, yet he'd felt something, sensed a communion he wanted to explore.

"All right, we've established that we know each other and that we're attracted. We're going to have to continue to make it look convincing. Are you going to have any problems with that?"

An enormous one, she thought, searching his handsome, angular face. But there was no way she would admit it to him.

"I suppose I've had less pleasant assignments," she drawled, using humor to defuse her own nervousness, while praying that her acting capabilities were up to the challenge.

"Thanks a lot."

"Well, you have to admit you asked for that one."

"What about a jealous boyfriend?" The thought had him unconsciously drawing his eyebrows into a frown.

"We're getting a little personal, aren't we?"

"I thought getting personal was the whole idea. At any rate, I already have enough of a reason to watch my back; I don't need to worry about getting in trouble for poaching."

"What a charming way to put it," she replied just as testily. "No, there's no one right now. But—how about you?"

He thought briefly of Madeline and the nasty scene that had ended things between them. "I haven't been seeing anyone for a while now. I'm surprised you don't know that, too."

Hearing the faint sarcasm in his voice, she decided that wouldn't do. "The only reason I knew about Allison and Bob is that I was doing a profile on you at the time. Stan had just recommended you to replace him," she said more warmly. "I wanted to make sure you were someone I could work with." She shrugged. "I watched you for a few days. The wedding just happened to be part of your itinerary that weekend. I haven't invaded your privacy since."

Nate studied her for a long moment, reminded again of how little he knew her. And yet, she'd just opened up to him in a way he would wager she rarely did with her other clients.

He inclined his head. "Sorry. I suppose I'm feeling a bit paranoid these days."

"Under the circumstances I suppose you're entitled."

"There's a benefit dinner on Friday," he said, his gaze caught by the lingering sheen of wine on her lips. "Would you like to proceed with this 'relationship' then?"

"Friday? Isn't there anything sooner?"

Amusement lit Nate's eyes as the desire to taste her again pulled him. Needing to do something with his hands, he lifted the rose from its vase and brought it close to inhale its fleeting scent. "Already can't bear the thought of our being apart, eh?"

"I *meant* we don't have the time to waste."

He gave her a wounded look. "Rennie, this might come as a surprise to you, but a party animal I'm not."

"Then you're just going to have to change your stripes."

"Your wish is my command," he drawled, drawing the flower across her cheek before placing it back in its vase.

Rennie shook her head, but couldn't quite hold back a smile. "Nate, will you be serious?"

"I thought I was supposed to be dazzled."

"Fine, but we need to talk business."

"Sorry, you're right." He sipped his drink, telling himself he had no right to be feeling so inanely pleased, considering the reason they were doing all this. "Let me check my calendar when I get back to the office. I'm sure there's some gathering going on that I'd been planning to avoid."

"You'll have to remember to fill me in on the

various dress codes. We don't want your peers to question your taste. I have a feeling a frantic shopping trip is in my immediate future.''

''Just think silk and send me the bills. Better yet, why don't I come along to give my expert opinion?''

Such generosity, she thought, ignoring the teasing gleam in his eyes. That was all she needed—him along with her as she went to buy evening attire and all those lacy bits of nothing that went beneath. ''Why don't we stick with my sending you the bills?''

''Killjoy,'' he grumbled. ''Are you going to give me some kind of background story on yourself so that when people ask me about you, I don't sound like I met you five minutes ago?''

''Good thinking...but that works both ways. I don't think it would be a good idea for your secretary to know more about your likes and dislikes than I do.'' Rennie made a mental note to draw up a personality chart for each of them to fill out when she got home. She was so involved with her own thoughts that it took her a few moments to notice Nate's troubled frown.

''What's wrong?''

''I just thought of something that puts a giant hole in our plans.''

''How giant?''

''Big enough to make me wonder if you're not going to dump this back in my lap.'' He polished off the rest of his drink and signaled the cocktail waitress for a refill. "Oh, hell. How do I put this delicately?"

"Never mind offending me, tell me what you're talking about."

"Being my lover—my *pretend* lover, that is— will give you the opportunity to meet the people I know on a social level, but not all of those that I deal with professionally."

"Are you saying I wouldn't be welcome to visit you at your office?"

"Exactly."

"That's crazy."

"Self-preservation. I've learned not to mix the two."

Rennie's answering look went from comprehending to sardonic. "Serves you right for not choosing your companions with more discretion."

"Now you sound like a properly jealous girlfriend."

"Stuff it, counselor."

"Yes, well...at any rate, I've grown adamant about keeping my personal and professional lives separate, and the point is that just taking you out with me and giving hints about us being an item isn't going to justify breaking my own rules. People would smell that something's not quite right."

"No wonder you've never married. Who'd

want to live with someone who made rules like that?''

"Oh, that's rich. I don't see a ring on your left hand, either.''

"At least *I* made the attempt once."

Nate stared, surprised. "I didn't know."

"It didn't make me a better detective so I left it off my résumé," she muttered, angry with herself for letting it slip.

As she looked away, Nate continued to stare at her, feeling as if he'd just had the wind knocked out of him; feeling an urge to fold her close for the hurt he heard beneath the cynicism.

Feeling.

The tumultuous eruption of emotions were more than he'd felt in a long time. And they were happening too quickly.

It didn't make sense, he told himself. He'd known her two years only to realize he didn't know her at all, and yet in a matter of an hour or two he was caught up in a crazy whirlwind of impulses and desires that couldn't be happening at a worse time.

The cocktail waitress returned with his drink and he gratefully took a deep swallow. "This is a helluva situation," he muttered.

"You're not going to get any arguments on that one from me." Rennie smoothed the napkin on her lap, determined to find a viable solution they could both work with. Damn, she thought.

She'd believed she had this all figured out. She should have known they would hit a glitch somewhere. "Well, short of my moving in with you, what do you suggest we do?"

"I'll have to—Bingo."

She glanced up. "Pardon?"

"Your suggestion…it's perfect."

"But I haven't made any—" She felt the blood drain from her face. *Oh, God.* "Are you crazy? Forget it. That wasn't a suggestion, that was comic relief. You know, my idea of a drastic measure."

"Don't my circumstances qualify as drastic?"

Not compared to what her situation would be if she agreed to what he was suggesting. "I think we need to look at something else."

"There *is* nothing else. Rennie, think about it. It's the only way people will believe the confirmed bachelor has really gone over the deep end. It would justify anything else I do—including inviting you to see my office, and wanting you to come pick me up for luncheon dates and whatever."

"We'll probably have this case solved before any of that's necessary anyway," Rennie replied, racking her brain for another idea. *Any* idea.

"But what if it's not?"

"We'll deal with that then!"

"That isn't your way of operating. You never

do things halfway or leave things open to chance. That's part of the reason I admire you so much.''

Right now she didn't want his admiration, and she *didn't* want to move in with him. Rennie closed her eyes, torn between wanting to help him and her instincts for self-preservation. She'd worked hard to rebuild her life after Fred's death and Alan's desertion. She didn't think she could risk becoming too involved with Nate.

"I can't just pick up my belongings and move in with you," she said, groping for the smallest bit of logic she could find. "I have a life of my own, other clients, a *cat*!"

"Did I mention I'm particularly good with children and small animals?"

"I don't want to hear this."

Nate watched as she massaged her temples with her fingertips. Her nails were short and unpolished, not at all like those of the women he usually dated. He knew he was asking for a lot. He also had no right to push her this way, but he had to make her understand that he trusted her as he trusted no one else.

"I need you, Rennie." Nate leaned toward her, his voice filled with urgency, his look compelling. "Granted, we're strangers in a lot of ways, but I think of you as a friend. If you can't see your way to accept this professionally, will you look at my case as a *friend* and reconsider?"

"That's dirty pool, Montgomery."

"Excuse me, sir. Your salad?"

As their waiter set Nate's salad before him, Rennie once again tried to collect herself, reminded that even now his blackmailer could be watching them. It wasn't likely, but if she'd learned one thing at the knee of Fred Paris, it was to expect the unexpected. She straightened and watched as the waiter ground fresh pepper over Nate's salad.

"Another wine, miss?"

"Please," she replied, dropping her gaze to what remained of hers. Suddenly she realized that this situation was affecting her far too strongly. She would stop at a second glass, of course, but the impulse to get very inebriated was there nonetheless.

When they were alone again, Nate pushed the salad aside and sat back to meet her resentful but resigned gaze. Slowly he released the breath he hadn't been aware of holding. "You're going to do it, aren't you? Even though you don't like the idea."

"That about sums it up, I guess."

"When do you think you can move in?"

Rennie's heart nosedived at merely the thought. "Ah…tomorrow? But forget what I said about my cat. I think it would be better if I leave her at home and have a neighbor check in on her when I can't."

"Afraid she might get too attached to me and won't want to leave?" Nate teased.

"Yeah," she muttered, annoyed that he was handling this far better than she. "Terrified."

"Rennie." Nate reached across the table to take her hand. For a moment they simply looked at each other, he wondering, she worrying. Then Nate lifted her hand to his lips and pressed a light kiss in her palm. "Thank you," he murmured.

Rennie could have hugged their waiter for choosing that moment to bring the rest of their lunch. But as she sat there eyeing her spinach salad, the sensation of Nate's lips on her skin continued to warm her palm.

So much for worrying that he might not be able to adapt to the situation, she thought fretfully. It looked as though Nate Montgomery was a man who could adapt all too well.

"I must be out of my mind," Rennie muttered Wednesday afternoon as she stood in the entryway of Nate's apartment and took her first look around. "Never mind worrying about Arabella liking this place too much; what about *me*?"

She put down her suitcase and tote bag, tossed the key Nate had left with the security guard downstairs onto the entry table and stepped into the living room. It was like entering a beautiful sanctuary, what with the walls and carpet radiating warmth in the same rich shade of burgundy.

As she ran her fingers along the back of the couch, dramatically upholstered in an indigo and burgundy Navajo print, she scanned the rest of the room. Dark-shaded brass lamps, finely polished side tables, deep chairs—all carefully arranged for both usefulness and visual appeal. She wouldn't have to ask to know that Nate liked to curl up with a book in the chair by the floor lamp, or that he enjoyed working at the huge mahogany desk by the sliding glass doors that led to the balcony. He might enjoy surrounding himself with fine things, but he also made use of them.

Unable to resist the impulse, she kicked off her sneakers and curled her toes into the plush carpeting. It beat the throw rugs on her hardwood floors any day. And the view, she thought, wandering over to the windows, was wonderful. Today Lake Michigan was relatively calm, but as anyone who lived on its banks knew, during a storm it could create swells that made you believe you were viewing an ocean.

A quick inspection of the rest of the apartment proved equally impressive. The kitchen was bright and had all the modern conveniences, suggesting Nate either enjoyed cooking or had a pampered housekeeper. Rennie hadn't asked about a housekeeper and made a mental note to do so.

Rennie snuck a peek at the large master bedroom—for a sense of the apartment's schematics, she assured herself—and quickly left, feeling Nate's presence more strongly in the dramatic and masculine room.

The guest room made her smile. At the moment it was more storage room than bedroom, where Nate apparently kept everything he didn't want to part with but otherwise had no use for. On the other side of a freshly made but uncovered full-size bed were boxes piled three and four high, some identified as things such as albums, others as receipts, and a few with the intriguing appellation of "tuit." She was glad to see he wasn't the complete perfectionist he appeared to be and, wondering if there was going to be room in the closet for her things, she went to retrieve her baggage.

When Nate walked in an hour later, he was immediately assaulted by the pulsating sounds of some unknown rock group rupturing the speakers of his stereo and a feminine voice down the hallway singing her heart out with the lead singer on the tape. He broke into a wry smile.

And he'd been worried that she would back out?

All morning and afternoon he'd been nervous, feeling like a groom who'd won his bride in a publisher's sweepstakes drawing. He'd questioned his sanity for inviting—no, *strongarming*—her to move in. He'd worried if he had remembered to empty some drawers for her in the guest room. He had wondered if his impulse to bring her flowers would be taken the wrong way. Because he couldn't decide how he meant the gesture himself, he'd picked up a chilled bottle of chardonnay instead, remembering her seeming preference for white wine.

He set the wine on the entryway table beside her key and went into the living room, promptly tripping over a pair of sneakers.

No doubt about it; Rennie was moving in.

The tape ended, but she kept singing. He followed the sound down the hallway to the guest room, where he found her gyrating to the song she was singing while placing a dress on a hanger. He leaned against the doorjamb, enjoying the view.

"Can't be nuthin' but what I am—aah!" She'd spotted him and muffled her scream by clapping her hand over her mouth. She quickly moved it to cover her heart. "Nate, you *fiend*, you scared me half to death!"

"Sorry," he said, not quite able to subdue his grin. "But don't stop on my account."

She opened her mouth to give him a suitable retort, then shut it, checking her watch instead. "What are you doing home this early?"

"I thought you might need some help moving in."

It wasn't fair, she thought, taking in his gray

three-piece suit. It wasn't fair that he could look so gorgeous and still make that crooked smile seem sweet. She, on the other hand, felt like the wrong end of a dust mop. Lifting her hair off her damp neck, she indulged in a fatalistic sigh.

"Thanks, but I was only taking the price tags off the rest of these things. You know, it's criminal what they charge for evening gowns these days, when they're about as substantial as a nightgown—and don't *ask* what they charge for those. You're going to regret giving me carte blanche."

Nate looked from the silky bronze gown she picked up to the fuchsia tank top that clung to her small, firm breasts and bet otherwise. "I guess they base their prices on the theory that less is more. I'm sorry about the boxes; I'm a little cramped for space these days."

"That's okay. But I did wonder...what's tuit?"

He stroked his chin. "I'll look through it when I get around to it." As she chuckled, he shrugged. "When my parents retired and moved to Florida, my mother decided I should reinherit everything that used to be in my old room."

"Florida, huh? That's something I should remember. Are you close?"

"I'm an only child; what do you think?"

"I doubt it needs much brain work," she said,

hanging the dress in the closet. "They probably spoiled you rotten."

"Probably, but I gave them a lot to work with." Nate loosened his tie, beginning to enjoy this. For the first time he noticed the pile of cosmetics on the dresser. They were all still in the manufacturers' original packaging. Sticking out from the bottom was a book on makeup techniques. He found the idea that she thought she needed help more endearing than amusing. "Did you have any problems getting the key from Wilson?"

Rennie thought of the stocky security guard downstairs and the way he'd blushed when she introduced herself, as Nate had directed her to the day before. She'd decided right there and then that Nate didn't often lend out his key. "No, but did you know he's expected to eat his lunch at his desk? He doesn't even get a coffee break in the afternoon. The man's responsible for the security of this entire building and he's a virtual prisoner in it. Nobody should have to work under those conditions—so I gave him a number to call."

"Why am I not surprised? I hope it wasn't Mario DePalma's," Nate added, watching her collect an odd assortment of shoes scattered on the floor only to toss them back into her suitcase.

"Very funny."

"What are you doing now?" She was down on all fours, peering under the bed.

"I've lost my sneakers."

"They're in the living room. We introduced ourselves to each other as I came in."

"Oh, no." Rennie plopped down on the carpet and gave him an apologetic look. "Maybe I'd better warn you that this is about as organized as I get. When I'm working, you can ask me for an address, a receipt and—" She snapped her fingers. "I know exactly where everything is; but the rest of the time... Last chance," she said almost hopefully. "Tell me to go or who knows, I might even bring the tenants' association down on your back."

Nate considered for a moment longer before stepping fully into the room. "You know what you need?" He extended his hand to her. When she took it, he easily pulled her to her feet. "You need a glass of wine and some mellow music to help you relax."

No, she told herself, she needed to have her head examined for letting herself get talked into this. But she let him lead her down the hallway anyway. Inevitably her sense of humor resurfaced. "Don't like my music, huh?"

"I might reconsider if I heard it played at a decibel where it wouldn't threaten to shake loose the fillings in my teeth. How do you feel about scampi?"

"As a name for a puppy or a musical group?"

"As a shrimp. The dish is a specialty of mine."

He wanted to *cook* for her? For a moment she had a vision of them sitting at the dining-room table, candlelight, him trying to feed her a bite from his plate. She rubbed her damp palms on the seat of her sweatpants. "Ah—don't take this wrong, but I think I'd prefer pizza."

He began to protest and then shrugged. One way or another there would be other dinners. "Pizza it is, then."

At the stereo, he removed her tape and replaced it with one of his. When he looked up, he saw she'd neatly placed her sneakers to the side and was reaching for the bag holding the wine. As she looked inside, he watched her tawny eyebrows lift.

"Are you sure you want to waste this on pizza?"

"It's not the food that makes a wine worthy, it's the company."

"Is that why I buy it by the jug?"

"Pardon?"

"Nothing."

As he crossed over to his desk and picked up the phone book, Rennie stood there at odds with what to do or say. She was beginning to realize this was going to be even more difficult than she'd thought.

"Thin crust or thick?" Nate asked as he dialed.

"Are you kidding? I have a small fortune invested in gorgeous new clothes. Make it thin."

He gave her a sweeping glance. "Thick. You can handle it. With the works."

"Oh, sure, why not," she drawled. "And while you're at it, tell them to really load up on the onions."

His laughter followed her all the way to the kitchen where she went to hunt down a corkscrew. A moment later she heard him give their order to the person on the other end of the line. "And *hold* the onions," she heard him add.

Some people, she decided, couldn't resist being cute.

Chapter Four

Nate drove into his office building's garage only to find the first level already crowded. "Guess we're going to be one of the last arrivals," he said, taking the circular drive down to the next level.

"I don't mind," Rennie replied, inwardly sighing as she noted all the luxury sedans that filled the second floor as well. The idea of slipping into the benefit unnoticed appealed to her. Far more than dealing with another open house like the one they went to the night before. She'd only urged Nate to go so that they wouldn't have to spend a second night alone at the condominium. That first evening, conversation and wine had flowed so easily they'd lost track of time and didn't get to bed until after midnight. It worried her that they were getting along so well.

Nate finally found a parking place on the third level and, turning off the engine, shifted to study her profile. "Don't tell me you're nervous? After last night? You had Marv Remington eating out of the palm of your hand."

"But Evelyn Remington kept giving me the third degree every time she succeeded in separating you and me. I'm not even sure I remember half the things I told her."

"Relax. I doubt she'll be here tonight, anyway."

She's probably the only one who isn't, Rennie thought, as Nate circled the car to open the door for her. She shook her head; last night they'd had words about *that* as well, and the memory brought a hint of laughter back to her eyes.

"You're supposed to be touched, not amused," Nate said, as she slid out.

"If we were back in the old days, and I had to wrestle yards of skirts plus a high carriage, I'd be more than touched, I'd be grateful. But pardner, them days is over."

Nate locked and shut the car door before taking her arm. "Then look at it this way, how am I going to convince anyone that I'm mad about you if I don't use any and every excuse to be near you?"

Rennie curled her lips into a near pout. "The client isn't supposed to be more perceptive than the investigator."

"That's my last insight of the evening," he said, giving her a wink. "From here on in I'm here purely as a decoy."

The word sent a cold chill racing down her spine. "Don't say that."

"It's what I feel like in this straitjacket."

"And it's a very attractive straitjacket," Rennie purred, trying to recapture their light mood. But inside she sighed. He looked so wonderful in his black formal wear. It gave him such an aristocratic elegance; she felt like Cinderella just walking beside him. Only the weight of the small automatic in her purse acted as a sobering reminder that this was no fairy tale.

At the elevator, Nate pushed the Up button before returning his attention to her. Once again he admired her sapphire velvet gown. "You're the one who looks terrific tonight. I particularly like this," he said, running his finger along the lovely ice-blue satin shawl collar that left her shoulders bare. "I'm tempted to do a case study to determine which is smoother, the satin or you."

Rennie could feel her heart leap against the starburst brooch that held satin to velvet. Luckily their elevator arrived and she was spared from having to think of an appropriate response. She was finding it more and more difficult to speak to Nate when they were alone. When they were among other people, it was easy. She felt safe playing her role of his new starry-eyed lover. But when they were alone, Nate didn't seem inclined to drop his performance, and how was she supposed to deal with that?

No, she amended with brutal honesty, she was concerned with how long she was going to be able to resist this change in him. With equally brutal discipline, she turned her thoughts to the event they were attending.

The benefit was a kickoff for the campaign to raise funds for a new children's clinic in the lower west side of the city. It was being held in the club at the top floor of Nate's office building. As Rennie and Nate stepped into the empty car, she was tempted to ask him if it would be possible to stop by his office, either now or before they left. She wanted to look around, see if she could get a feel for anything, learn the layout of the office. But before she had a chance, the elevator stopped for more passengers at the lobby level.

"Nate! What timing," said the heavyset man with the receding hairline, as he escorted his own companion into the car. "We decided to take a cab. You know my night vision's bad enough without all this rain. Who's this lovely lady?"

Nate slid his hand around Rennie's waist and gave her a slight, but reassuring squeeze. "Darling, this is my partner, Wendell Dillard, and his long suffering wife, Margarett."

"Oh, Nate," Maggie gasped, lifting a gloved

hand to her lips and glancing at the other people who'd entered with them. "You're terrible."

"But accurate," her husband added, punctuating the remark with the cigar he'd failed to put out when he entered the car.

"Wendell, Maggie, I'd like you to meet the best thing that's happened to me since I passed the bar exam. Rennie Paris."

"Uh-oh. That sounds serious," Wendell said with a lift of his slashing salt-and-pepper eyebrows. "I didn't know you were seeing anyone since you and Madeline, er—" He suffered an elbow to the ribs from Maggie. "Sorry."

"That's all right," Rennie said, extending her hand to him and slipping into the story she'd rehearsed. "Nate and I have talked about our time apart. You see, we met at the wedding of mutual friends a few years ago." She shook hands with Maggie Dillard. "And even though my career took me away from Chicago for a while, once our paths crossed again it was as if we'd never been separated."

"How romantic," Maggie replied. "What do you do, Miss Paris?"

"Please call me Rennie. I was a model— mostly catalogue work. As you can see, I'm not quite tall enough for the runways."

"How glamorous."

"Not as much as I'd hoped. That's why I decided to come back to Chicago. An old friend is opening a boutique in the State Street market-place area. She wants me to be her partner.''

"And I'm trying to convince her to be mine instead,'' Nate said. When he saw Rennie's startled reaction, he quickly brushed his lips against her forehead. "Poor darling, it can't be a surprise to you?''

"Nate,'' she said, managing a shaky laugh. "You'll embarrass Mr. and Mrs. Dillard.''

"Not at all,'' Wendell replied, beaming at both of them. "We're not so old that we don't remember what it was like to fall in love, eh, Maggie? But if our Nate here is half as convincing as I know he can be, you'd better drop that Mr. and Mrs. nonsense.''

The elevator arrived at the top floor and they exited to find the lobby area crowded. Music from a small combo playing on the raised stage inside the club competed with the conversations going on around them, creating a din that made any serious communication impossible.

"Why don't you take Rennie and Maggie inside and see if you can find our firm's table,'' Wendell said in a raised voice to Nate. "I've just remembered a phone call I neglected to make.''

"Oh, Wendell,'' Maggie replied. "Not again. Can't you forget about business for one evening?''

"In a minute, dear.''

As he shuffled toward the phones at the far end

of the lobby, his wife turned to apologize to Rennie and Nate. Nate cut her off with a dismissive shake of his head.

"Forget it, Maggie. We've both known him for too many years not to know he's happiest when he's working."

"But he's been so tired lately, and he *did* admit to me tonight that his doctor's warned him to slow down."

Nate glanced back at Wendell. They'd never been as close as he and Hank Collins had been, but he had a good working relationship with his surviving partner. "I'll have a talk with him if you like. But right now let's see if we can find that table."

From fluorescent lights and buff-colored walls, they stepped into candlelight and the mellow shades of mauve and gray. As they followed a hostess, who checked their names off a list and was leading them to their table, they were hailed a number of times by people already seated.

After one—more polite than friendly—exchange, Rennie slowed down slightly to whisper to Nate. "Who was the man with the redhead?"

"Assistant DA. Name's Prather."

"He doesn't like you."

"The feeling's mutual. Here's another fan."

There were a few people already sitting at their table, but Rennie didn't have to guess who Nate had made the reference to when she was introduced to Albert Dillard, Maggie and Wendell's son. He was a taller, gaunt-faced version of his father, but the greetings he and Nate exchanged, though civil, had none of the magnanimity she'd sensed with Wendell. Rennie shook hands with him and found his limpid, then forced herself to give his sullen-looking wife a pleasant smile. Whatever her personal feelings, she couldn't afford to start the evening off by making enemies.

Nate neatly maneuvered Maggie to sit beside her son and placed Rennie on his left. "Champagne or dance?" he whispered into her ear.

"Dance. I already have some questions."

Luckily the song being played was a slow one. Leading her to the crowded dance floor, Nate drew Rennie into his arms. "Let me guess. You want to ask me about Albert?"

"Besides jealousy, what does he have against you?"

"I refuse to accept him as a partner in the firm."

"Because of his father?"

"Because he's an incompetent, and a wimpy one at that."

Rennie couldn't help but smile at the accurate description. "Don't get personal; not everyone can have your charisma."

Nate didn't bother hiding his pleasure and tucked her closer. "Is that what I have?"

"And don't fish. I think you're getting a swollen head as it is with my fawning over you like a lovesick puppy."

His answering laugh was low and tickled her ear. "Yes, dear."

"Good evening, Montgomery. It doesn't look like you let the grass grow under your feet for very long."

Rennie felt Nate stiffen and turned to the prematurely silver-haired man dancing with a petite blonde beside them. The cold look in the other woman's topaz eyes made her otherwise doll-like face less attractive and put Rennie immediately on her guard.

"McGraw. Hello, Madeline." Nate went through quick introductions. "What brings you here? I thought you saved your patronage for the arts."

"Lew and I needed an excuse to celebrate our latest coup." Madeline edged her body closer to her partner's and gave him a seductive smile. "Didn't we, pet?"

"That's what I believed when you first told me you wanted to come here," the older man said, but there was no missing the annoyance in his voice.

For an instant Madeline's smile faltered. "Don't listen to him," she said brightly. "He doesn't like to write any kind of check that isn't to himself. The truth is we're celebrating the sale of the Briarly building by Grant Park.''

"Congratulations. Lewis and Madeline were the brokers who helped us sell our former location before we moved here," Nate told Rennie.

Madeline gave a throaty laugh. "Why Nate, how tidy you make it sound. The least you could do is add that it was the beginning of a long and very satisfying relationship."

Lew's tight smile flattened into an even grimmer line. "I think it's time we returned to our champagne, Maddy." He nodded curtly to Nate and Rennie. "See you around."

As she watched them walk away, Rennie noticed the sequins on the curvaceous blonde's gown and couldn't help comparing them to glittering icicles. So *that* was the woman she was pretending to have replaced. "Fascinating couple.''

"He's a bad influence on her."

"Really? If you ask me, it's the other way around."

"You don't understand," Nate replied wearily.

Rennie looked up to see that he was still watching the couple. Or rather Madeline, she corrected herself. The troubled expression caused a painful wrenching within her chest. She had a feeling she understood all too well.

"I think we could use a drink, too," she said, carefully extricating herself from his arms.

Not needing another taste of reality to remind her why she was there, Rennie focused on the job she'd been hired to do.

Mingling turned out to be easier than she'd expected. Occasionally she found the background she and Nate had devised for her tested, but because she'd been careful to keep it as close to her own as possible, she answered the discreet inquiries smoothly. No, she would say, she had no family living. Yes, she met Nate at a wedding—though in truth she'd never actually spoken to him—and yes, they'd known each other for two years. By the time she excused herself and slipped off to freshen up in the powder room, she was relatively pleased with the practiced breeziness she'd effected, bringing to life the vivacious and obviously infatuated young woman she was supposed to be.

"Oh, I suppose she's attractive in a unique sort of way," Madeline Brookes was saying as Rennie entered the lounge. "Heaven knows she's shapeless enough to be a model. But you're never going to convince me that Nate's actually serious about her." She sniffed delicately. "If he took her to bed, he'd deserve a Purple Heart for all the splinters he'd get."

"Maddy, I heard from a reliable source that

she's moved *in* with him," the woman beside her whispered.

At that moment Madeline spotted Rennie and she gave her a venomous look. But the confrontation Rennie expected never occurred. Nate's ex simply dropped her lipstick back into her evening bag and haughtily walked out. Her companion followed, giving Rennie an embarrassed smile.

Well, it could have been worse, Rennie told herself as she took a seat at the end of the vanity mirror. But she had to wonder how Nate could have cared for a woman like that. "Well, nobody said this was going to be easy," she muttered to herself as she hunted in her bag for her lip gloss.

"Pardon?"

Rennie looked up to find Albert's wife, Faith, standing beside her. She gestured dismissively. "Sorry. I was just talking to myself."

"I was going to ask you what you thought of our big happy family, but if they've already driven you to doing that, I guess I have my answer."

Her voice was edged with cynicism, but Rennie pretended not to notice. She already had a few hunches about Faith Dillard, and on how to treat her. "They're not a bad group. It's just that I prefer more intimate dinner parties than these kinds of gatherings."

Faith gave her a doubtful look before grimacing at her own reflection in the mirror. "Why did I ever buy this dress? I look like one of the frumpy sisters in a Jane Austen novel.''

"The color is too bland for you, that's all.''

"You think so?''

Rennie heard the wistfulness in her voice and knew she'd found the opening she'd been looking for. "Sure. With your dark hair and olive complexion you're better off wearing jewel-tone colors. You have very pretty eyes. Something in a blue like this would be great on you. And if you had your hair cut...to about here—'' she indicated chin length "—it would give your fine hair more body. I'll bet Albert would hardly recognize you.''

"He doesn't pay much attention to me these days as it is.'' With a sigh, Faith sat down on the stool beside Rennie's. "You must think I'm a real witch, or at least a basket case.''

"What I think is that you're unhappy and that there's something troubling you. Do you want to talk about it?''

Faith gave her a dry smile. "Got about six months?''

"We could have lunch sometime.''

"Did I ever misjudge you.'' Faith shook her head. "My first impression was that you were a self-centered airhead. You know, the stereotypical glamour girl? But you're not. You're okay.''

"Thanks...I think.''

"I guess I should warn you; I have an aversion

for beating around the bush, too. I figure my husband and father-in-law do enough of that for the entire family and then some. The price of being married to an attorney.''

"You don't sound very enthusiastic about your husband's choice of professions,'' Rennie said, dropping her voice as a few women joined them.

Faith opened her clutch purse, drew out her cigarettes and a lighter and lit one. "If I thought he was happy, I'd do handsprings. But all he's doing is fulfilling his father's dream. 'Daddy' wanted him to follow in his footsteps, so dutiful Albert responded accordingly.'' She exhaled a long stream of smoke and a wry smile almost transformed her face into that of a girl again. "When we met in college, he wanted to be an analyst. He's a great listener,'' she insisted, seeing Rennie's surprise. "To everyone but me that is.''

"Because you're a reminder of what he didn't fight for?'' Rennie asked gently.

"You're too quick for me.'' As quickly as she lit it, Faith crushed her cigarette and waved her hand to disperse the smoke hovering around them. "I'm trying to give these things up. Can you tell?'' She began to rise, but stopped when Rennie touched her arm.

"Let's have that lunch.''

The two women eyed each other for a moment. There was a hesitation in Faith's eyes that Rennie could easily read. "You're afraid liking me and trusting me will backfire and only make things harder for Albert," she said kindly. "On the other hand, you're afraid that I might get the wrong idea and think you're trying to use me to put in a good word for him with Nate."

"I guess you don't beat around the bush much, either, do you?"

"I'm not overly fond of it, no."

Faith nodded, respect warming her eyes. "How about next week? I do a few hours of reading to senior citizens at a nursing home on Tuesdays and Thursdays. It's near the university off Taylor."

"I know it. Do you know the soup-and-salad place a block up from there?"

"Are you kidding? There's a booth there that practically has my name on it. How's Thursday sound? Noon?"

"Tuesday's better. It would give you less time to think about canceling."

This time Faith almost laughed. "Maybe you should have been an analyst yourself."

"My life is full enough as it is," Rennie said, standing. "Come on, I'll keep you company going back to our table."

Before they'd left for the benefit, Nate and Rennie had agreed not to stay the whole evening. When she and Faith returned to their table, Nate had just returned from dancing with Maggie. She discreetly signaled him that she was ready to leave if he was, but he surprised her by leading her to the dance floor instead.

"I've barely had the chance to dance with you this evening," he told her as he drew her close. "And don't forget, we have a reputation to uphold."

"Nice of you to remember," she drawled, before she could stop herself.

"What's that supposed to mean?"

She could have kicked herself for that slip, but now that it was out, she decided to follow up on it. "I would have preferred your being honest with me about Madeline, that's what it means. Look, it's none of my business if you two still have something going between you. But when it effects my credibility, I do care. Aside from looking like a fool, I don't like wasting my time."

"What are you talking about? I haven't done anything—"

"I *saw* you earlier having that cozy chat with her, Nate."

He was quiet a moment before exhaling heavily. "I'm sorry for that, but one thing it *wasn't* was cozy. The fact is Madeline has some serious problems and even though we're no longer involved, I can't help but be concerned for her."

"If this story gets any sadder, you're going to have to lend me a hanky."

"It's over, Rennie," he insisted. When she failed to respond, he tilted his head to study her expression, then broke into a wry smile. "You know what I think? You're jealous."

"Of Miss Transylvania? Dream on."

"What good is logic when the green-eyed monster strikes?" He bent his head to whisper in her ear. "But more than that, I think you're angry with yourself for discovering that you're jealous. Would it help to know that I rather like the idea?"

"I'm going to ignore you until you change the subject."

"Why so testy all of a sudden?"

How dare he laugh at her! How dare he find her vulnerability to him amusing! "Can we please leave now?" she asked stiffly.

"In a minute." Didn't she understand that he'd been wanting an excuse to hold her again like this?

The combo slipped from one slow number into another, and Nate decided if he couldn't make her see, perhaps he could make her feel. He drew her closer yet and placed her hand against his chest. Then he moved his own hand beneath the heavy fall of her hair to caress her nape. The skin there was warm and softer than velvet. "Tickle?" he asked, feeling her stiffen.

"A little," she lied. "Nate, you needn't over-do it."

"I disagree. I'm trying to redeem myself to my friend, but she's resisting believing in me. Resisting me, period. Why is that, I wonder?"

"We have a business deal. Nothing more."

"That's not true," he replied, continuing the gentle massage. "It stopped being true the moment you threw your arms around me and I kissed you at the club."

She began to protest but his caress stopped her cold. "Oh, God, that feels good," she moaned softly.

Though she'd discriminately sipped her way through only a glass and a half of champagne, she was suddenly overcome with a desire that contradicted her protests. She wanted the moment, the man, the intimacy. It had been a long time since she'd allowed herself to get close to anyone. Need was like a dried thistle stinging her flesh. Tonight the pain was impossibly acute.

Nate heard her sigh and felt her slowly begin to relax against him. So many layers of clothes remained between them, and yet he was profoundly aware of the change her body telegraphed to his. "This is much nicer than arguing," he said, touching his cheek to hers.

"This could lead to trouble," she corrected—but only halfheartedly.

"And the polar ice cap is melting. Give it a rest, Paris."

She couldn't quite contain a soft chuckle. "I

should never have taken you on as a client. You're a hopeless optimist.''

"I like you, too." She was so willowy and sleek. Like a cat. The analogy made his smile broader. "What is your cat's name?"

She decided to stop trying to follow his line of thinking. "Arabella. Sometimes I call her Belle. Sometimes worse things. Why the sudden interest?"

"She's something we haven't talked about. Did you choose her or vice versa?"

At least he understood cats. "A little of both. I'd just moved back into Fred's old place and my neighbor, Mrs. Kinney, was about to move into a nursing home; she had Alzheimer's. Belle was her cat and we'd spent a lot of time together in the past. Taking her in seemed the least I could do to give Mrs. Kinney some peace of mind."

"Anyone ever tell you you're a softy, lady?"

Rennie closed her eyes, relishing this moment of tenderness, but her mind wouldn't quite shut down. "It's not an asset in my business."

"Nobody works twenty-four hours a day," he replied. He closed his eyes at the involuntary, sexy little moan she made as a result of his ministrations and wondered if she would make the same sound if he kissed her, or brought her body more completely against his. Their location made the former impossible, but with only the slightest adjustment, he succeeded in the latter.

Her breath caught in her throat. "Nate."

"Just for a moment, Rennie."

"It's wrong."

How could anything that felt this good be wrong? She fit against him so well. She might not want to accept it, but the truth was inescapable.

Beneath her hand, she felt the strong beat of his heart. His touch was possessive as he continued to caress her nape. For a moment longer she allowed herself the luxury of feeling, of being desired; she was too human to deny herself entirely. Then she gently pushed against his chest and drew back to look up at him.

"It's getting late and I have a full day tomorrow," she said, feeling her resolution take a blow at what she clearly read in his eyes. She took a calming breath. "Maybe we'd better leave."

He was tempted to draw her back into his arms, pressure her into admitting she wasn't as controlled as she wanted him to believe. But he sensed it would be a mistake.

Slow down, he cautioned himself, escorting her back to their table. He'd made a giant leap in getting closer to her tonight. If he wanted to learn why she was so skittish, if he wanted to find out why she was resisting him, he was going to have to be patient.

They said their good-nights and made their way out of the club. There were other couples waiting for elevators, but they were part of a group and when two elevators arrived simultaneously, they went in one, leaving the other for Nate and Rennie.

"Well, I noticed you weren't exactly a wallflower tonight," he drawled, punching the color-coded button for the garage floor and turning back to her.

Relieved that he wasn't going to continue with what had begun on the dance floor, Rennie allowed a slight smile. "I'm this week's novelty. You, on the other hand, have made your share of enemies."

"It comes with the territory."

"It makes my job harder."

"Tell me about it."

"Everyone I met tonight seems to agree that you're a very good attorney, but they have various reasons to resent you. For instance, the assistant DA, Prather? I spoke to him—"

"You *what*?" He didn't think he liked the idea of Prather being anywhere near her. "I thought the idea of all this was to be subtle."

"Oh, calm down, I was. In fact he thought it amusing that I should be so protective of you."

"Protective? What did you do?"

"What any infatuated woman would do when she notices someone shooting nasty looks at her man; I went over to ask him why and defended you—quite charmingly, too, I might add. Anyway, I discovered that you've made him look somewhat foolish in court during your last two meetings.''

''If the man leaves himself open to ridicule during his cross-examinations, why not?''

''I don't know. I wasn't there. All I'm saying is that his dislike for you is strong, but though he's hell-bent on getting back at you, I'm fairly sure it will be on the same turf.''

''Meaning?''

''Meaning, I don't think he belongs on the top of my list of suspects, though I won't rule him out entirely. However, if I were you, I'd make sure I did my homework next time I knew I had to face him in court.''

Nate chuckled softly. ''Yes, ma'am. What else did you learn?''

That Madeline isn't over you, either. But that really wasn't any of her business, was it? She forced herself to think of something else that might interest him. ''Albert doesn't seriously want to be a partner at the firm.''

Nate straightened. ''My, my. You have had a busy evening. But this time, I think you've been fed a line.''

''Maybe, but are you aware that he always wanted to be a shrink?''

''Says who?''

''Faith.''

The elevator chimed its arrival at their floor

and the doors slid open. Nate followed Rennie out. "She hasn't said more than a few dozen words to me in all the years since Albert joined the firm, and suddenly she's opening up to you?"

Rennie shivered, feeling the damp, cold air, and wished she hadn't left her coat in the car. "She's not that bad. She's—Nate, you don't have to do that." He'd removed his dinner jacket and was placing it over her shoulders. "Now *you'll* be cold."

"I'll turn the heater on in the car. Go on with what you were saying."

"I just wanted to tell you that I think a lot of her frigidness stems from how unhappy she and Albert are." When an engine started behind them, she glanced over her shoulder. She hadn't remembered seeing anyone else walking to their car. "She thinks he's making himself miserable trying to fulfill Wendell's own ambitions for him."

"Good. Then he won't be disappointed the next time his name comes up for partnership consideration and I reject it again. At any rate, I don't know what that has to do with my problem."

"Nothing, I suppose, but I wanted you to know. I liked Faith once we started talking," she added. "In fact, we're going to have lunch— Nate! Look out!"

She'd heard the car begin to ease out of its slot

and was prepared to step out of the way with Nate so it could pass. But suddenly the driver gunned the engine and headed straight for them.

Without thinking of her own safety, she pushed Nate out of the way. Then she threw her body in the opposite direction.

"Rennie!"

Nate's shout and the roaring engine reverberated in the garage. He felt a flash of pain in his side as he landed against the hood of a Mercedes, but ignored it and twisted in time to see Rennie disappear behind the car racing by. In seconds it had gone up the exit ramp.

He pushed himself off the car and ran to where she lay half-sprawled on the concrete floor.

"Did you get the license plate number?" she asked him breathlessly.

"What? No. Good God, I was concerned about *you*."

"It would have been handy. The windows were tinted so I couldn't see who was behind the wheel." She blew her hair out of her face before giving him a dry look. "Maybe we better read that note again. I thought that character said he wanted you out of town, not dead!"

"That's not funny," Nate said, feeling reaction set in. To keep his hands from trembling he grasped her by the shoulders. "You little fool! Do you realize that by pushing me out of the way, you almost got yourself killed?"

Well, of all the ungrateful jerks, she thought. She shrugged off his hands. "Just what do you think my job *is*?"

"To uncover information, *not* to be my bodyguard!"

"Aha! My mistake. Next time a car comes barreling down at you, I'll just step aside and say, 'Sorry. That's not in my job description,' and let you get creamed. Ouch! Damn it—"

She'd tried to straighten her leg and discovered she'd bruised it worse than she'd thought; and to top it all off, not only had she split the front seam of her gown, but she'd landed in a patch of oil.

Nate watched her struggle with her skirt while trying to inspect its damage. But her attempts at retaining some sense of demureness were a losing battle. By the time he had her on her feet, the legs he'd admired before were indelibly branded in his memory, from slim ankle to sleek thigh, and she was flinging oaths at him saltier than anything Long John Silver ever used.

"Rennie, will you just calm down? Will you— Oh, to hell with it," he muttered, locking his mouth to hers.

Suddenly his anger was forgotten, and his amusement. In its place came a different passion, hot and aching. He slipped his hands through her hair intent on exploring it. Her taste was no milder than her temperament. Rich. Heady. He thrust his tongue deep and lost himself.

For the second time in minutes, Rennie felt her

legs threaten to fail her. She felt herself being dragged under a whirlpool of emotions. Needs so long denied suffocated her, made her grip his shirt in desire and panic. That was the only reason she was momentarily incapable of stopping him, she assured herself. It wasn't *him*. It couldn't be him.

"Stop it!" She managed to pull away, wobbled and backed into a car, but decided it could be used for support. She half expected Nate to come after her and when he didn't, she narrowed her eyes suspiciously. "You had no right to do that."

"It's between us, Rennie. Ignoring it isn't going to make it go away."

Oh, he had nerve. Did he expect her to warm his bed while he worked out his problems with Madeline? "Take me home, please," she said, stiffly turning toward his car.

Maybe it was the best idea, he thought, retrieving his jacket from where it had fallen. They were both too tense right now; there was nothing he could say that wouldn't make things worse, because all he could think about was that he wanted her. She'd just saved his life by risking her own; some nut out there might be trying to kill him, and he wanted her.

"Fine job, Montgomery," he muttered to himself as he headed back toward her. If she didn't walk out on him, it wouldn't be because he didn't deserve it. "Start praying, pal."

Chapter Five

"I think that about covers this meeting's agenda," Wendell Dillard said, glancing around the boardroom table at the half dozen men and women facing him. He rested his gaze on Nate who sat at the opposite end of the table, staring off into space. "Do you have anything to add, Nate? How's Jerome versus Morgan Towers? Nate?"

"Hmm?" He stared at Wendell for a moment before realizing what he'd been asked. To his chagrin, he found that everyone else in the room was staring back at him. "Sorry," he muttered, with a self-deprecating smile. "I guess I was preoccupied."

"Am I the only one who thinks the weekend was long enough?" Wendell asked, softening the sarcasm in his voice with a faint smile.

Everyone around the table murmured affirmatively, except Nate. The truth was, although Wendell couldn't know it, Nate couldn't agree with his partner more. It had been a thoroughly rotten weekend, and the way things looked, Monday wasn't promising to be any better.

"Ah, Jerome versus Morgan Towers..." He struggled to think of something halfway worthy to report. "I've agreed to an out-of-court meeting, counsel only of course, and it's scheduled for Wednesday."

Wendell looked slightly startled for a moment before sitting back in his chair to digest the news. "An interesting development considering their original position. Was the gesture instigated by us or them?"

"Them. It could mean nothing, but I have a hunch they'll make an offer. However, I'll also bet it won't be enough to persuade our client to drop his suit."

"I know I don't have to remind you that you're dealing with a powerful group of people there."

Tell me about it, Nate thought, inclining his head. Powerful enough to destroy people's lives as well as their careers. But Rennie was convinced DePalma and his people were legitimate this time around.

At the thought of Rennie, his mood grew even more dejected. He was barely conscious of Wen-

dell adjourning the meeting, or of the others collecting their things and heading to their offices.
He closed his own notebook and rose, not even
noticing Wendell coming toward him until the
older man laid a hand on his shoulder.

"Nate, are you all right?"

"Of course. Fine. A little preoccupied maybe,
but—"

Wendell bowed his head, his jowls doubling
as they rested on his starched shirt and conservative tie. "I understand. It's personal and you
have every right to tell me to mind my own business."

Guilt made Nate hesitate in stepping around
his partner as he would normally have done.
Granted, he had an appointment in a few minutes,
and he and Wendell rarely saw eye to eye on
things—the least of them being Albert—but there
was no ignoring their long history together.

"Personal. Well, yes, but not in the way
you're obviously thinking." He rubbed the back
of his neck and swore under his breath. "Oh,
hell, I suppose you deserve to know since it could
ultimately effect you. I'm being blackmailed."

"Good Lord. How? *Why?*"

"Damned if I know. Look, I can't really go
into details right now. It might jeopardize the investigation."

"Then you've called in the police?"

"No, I'm using a private investigator. The

method the blackmailer is using compromises more people than myself and I thought bringing in the police at this point would raise the risk of media involvement. I'm hoping to avoid that.'' Nate's expression grew more grim. ''But I'm not sure I can for much longer. After Rennie and I left the benefit Friday, someone tried to run us over downstairs in the garage.''

''They *what*?'' Wendell stepped back to steady himself by gripping the table. Gray-faced, he looked away and shook his head. ''I don't know what to say. Good heavens, Rennie—''

''She's fine. She fell and bruised her leg, but she's not the type to be kept down for long.''

''Good, good...but for this to happen just when you two have found each other again. It's tragic.''

Nate didn't have to pretend to look grim. It was the other reason he was feeling as he did. He was beginning to regret he'd involved Rennie in this mess. Aware of what a strong family man Wendell was, he was tempted to confide her real identity to him—not to mention his deepening feelings toward her. God, if he didn't talk to someone soon, he was going to go crazy. But then he remembered Rennie's own insistence that no one else know what they were doing.

''Well, you *have* to call the police,'' Wendell said, upon recovering from his shock. ''That's all there is to it.''

"I can't. If it was only me involved with this, I wouldn't hesitate. But this concerns pictures, Wendell, and a lady's reputation. She's married."

"Not Rennie?"

"No, someone else, but the pictures are fakes."

"I see."

"You don't, but I don't really have time to explain. The point is that this blackmailer wants me out of Chicago."

"Why?"

Nate's laugh was mirthless. "There's the question of the hour. But I promise you, I'm going to find out."

Wendell straightened, and gripped Nate's hand. "What can I do to help?"

"Thanks for the offer, but there's nothing. Just be careful yourself." Nate checked his watch. "I'm sorry, I have to get back to my office. My appointment is probably already waiting for me. Listen, you realize this has to be kept confidential? Not even Maggie can be told about it."

"No, no, of course not, but Nate, we have to talk."

"Later."

She should have phoned to tell him she was coming and to wait for her, Rennie thought, as she walked into the offices of Dillard, Collins,

Montgomery and Associates. It was just after twelve and she'd probably missed him.

She followed the receptionist's directions to his office deciding that if he was out, maybe she could convince his secretary to tell her where he'd gone. Agnes seemed like a pleasant woman from what she'd perceived during their brief phone conversations. Motherly, but with a dry sense of humor. Shrewd, too, she thought, recalling how Agnes had picked up the similarity between her voice and that of the mystery lady who occasionally left messages for Nate.

"Hello," the middle-aged woman said, hanging up the phone as Rennie stopped before her desk. She glanced down at her appointment calendar before giving her a cautious smile. "Can I help you?"

"I hope so, Agnes. You could tell me he hasn't left for lunch yet. I'm Rennie."

"Yes, you are! Now I recognize your voice. Well, how nice to meet you in person. And you're in luck. He's been behind schedule all morning and he's still—"

"Agnes, did I hear—? Rennie."

She braced herself against the rush of nervousness she felt as Nate stepped out of his office and spotted her. They hadn't had an easy weekend, though other business had helped keep her away for most of it, and they'd argued when she'd returned Sunday evening. This morning he'd left for work before she finished showering.

Help me through this, she told him with her eyes.

Come here and I will.

They would have had to ask Agnes which of them made the first move. They only felt their own reaction, that strange pulling, like a magnet that drew them together.

"I should have called."

"You're always welcome, I told you that."

"I was running errands and was nearby."

"I'm glad." He lifted his hand to her cheek.

She hesitantly covered it with her own. For a moment they forgot their roles and their anger, and were caught up in the magic of what they saw in each other's eyes. It was the most natural thing for Nate to lower his head and touch his lips to hers. The most natural thing for her to kiss him back.

Sweet and painful emotion rose in him. He raised his head, smiled and drew her into his office.

As the door closed behind them, Agnes sighed, chewed on the end of her pen for a moment and then reached for her phone. After three rings she had a connection.

"Harvey? Honey, what were you planning to do for lunch?"

Behind the door, Nate leaned against it, his

gaze still locked with Rennie's. But when he tried to draw her toward him, she held back and slowly shook her head.

"Nate, wait. I didn't mean for us to—I don't know why I just did that. The last thing I wanted to do was give you the impression anything had changed."

He felt as if someone had just thrown ice water on him, and stared at her as she backed into one of the leather chairs and then moved around it to place it between them. She looked so fresh, so vibrant in her red blazer; it emphasized the honey color of her hair. He could almost feel its silky texture on his fingertips, and only pride allowed him the willpower not to follow her.

"Then why did you come?"

To buy time in order to regain her confidence—not to mention her equilibrium—she inspected his office. Like his home, it was sophisticated but serviceable and decorated in shades of gray. She thought that somewhat appropriate considering that's what the law had always seemed like to her, the law and life. Things were rarely clear-cut; nothing was easily explained.

"I have some news. I've made some headway this morning, and I thought you'd want to know."

That explained the excitement he'd seen in her eyes. *Fool, you'd believed it was for you.* He smoothed the hair at his nape. "Thank you. I do. Are you hungry?"

"Not really." She'd only had a sweet roll for breakfast, but that didn't mean she would be able to swallow a bite of anything if it meant sitting across the table from him.

"Me, neither. We'll take a drive to one of the parks then."

Agnes was gone when they came back out, which was just as well, Rennie thought. It would be hard to explain why they were suddenly taking pains *not* to touch each other. Nate scribbled a quick message to her, signaled one of the secretaries down the hall that he was leaving and then escorted Rennie out the side entrance.

"How's the leg?" he asked her, cutting his steps to half their normal stride.

"Fine." The bruise wasn't pretty, and she'd opted to wear slacks today, but it wasn't interfering with her mobility. "How was your morning?"

"Well, no one left me a note in my car and I didn't get run over," he muttered as they entered the garage. "So I suppose I must have had a terrific morning."

"The sarcasm isn't necessary, Nate."

"I don't know, I'm rather enjoying it."

Rennie bit her lip and waited for him to unlock the car. She wished she could think of something to say to put things back the way they were, but she knew that was impossible. After that kiss the other night, their relationship had crossed a strategic point and now nothing could ever be the same again.

"We can just sit here if you like," she told him when he settled behind the steering wheel.

Obviously she was having less difficulty with this situation than he was. "I feel like driving," he said briskly. "But go ahead and tell me your news."

She bit back the equally cool remark on the tip of her tongue and buckled her seat belt. "It's about the pictures and Karyn Jerome. I talked with her this morning and—"

"You called Karyn?"

"No, I went to see her."

Nate almost rear-ended a Cadillac at the cashier's booth. "Are you mad? Without even checking with me first?"

"Since when am I expected to clear things like that with you?"

He knew her feelings about a client interfering with an investigation, but this case was an exception. "What was the point, Rennie? What she does in her private life is of no concern to us. What was the point of humiliating the woman?"

Rennie had to wait for him to show his pass to the cashier before she could answer, but once they were out in the street and his window was rolled up, she replied just as heatedly. "She wasn't humiliated because she wasn't the woman in the photos.''

"Oh, great. What, she said so and you believe her?''

"I believed you, didn't I?''

"But not much else I've said,'' he muttered under his breath.

"Excuse me?''

"I said, maybe I jumped to conclusions. Go on.''

"To make a long story short, she has a rose tattoo on a strategic part of her anatomy, and if the photographer was trying to prove authenticity, you can bet that tattoo would be there—if he'd known about it. It's not her,'' she repeated almost smugly.

"She *showed* you?''

"Let's say Mrs. Jerome isn't quite the demure lady you led me to believe.''

Nate cleared his throat and turned south onto Lakeshore Drive. It was a cool, but sunny, day. The wind was brisk, buffeting the car and he had to hold the steering wheel with both hands. "So it wasn't either of us in those pictures. That doesn't get us any closer to the blackmailer.''

"No, but my other information does.'' She turned toward him. "After I left Karyn, I checked in with my service. There was a call from De-Palma.''

"This story is getting worse by the minute.''

"Will you please let me finish? I called him and he told me he'd located the photographer who doctored the pictures!" She nodded eagerly when he shot her a dubious look. "I went to see him. That is, Rocco and I went to see him."

"*Rocco?*"

"I know, but that's another story entirely. Just try to understand that Mr. DePalma decided it would be in my best interests to have him along. He thought the man might not talk to a woman alone. I was actually grateful to have him, Nate. The man took one look at Rocco and began to sing like a spring robin. Where are you going?"

He turned onto Jackson, a street that ran just north of Grant Park. He wasn't sure where he wanted to go, but suddenly he decided it might not be a good idea to stop in a park after all. He didn't think he trusted himself with having both hands free at the moment.

"Just finish the story," he ground out.

"There's not much more to tell. The photographer said that the man who ordered the work was a real creep. Tall, skinny. Not the type who could afford the fee it would cost to do the pictures. But he paid cash up-front and said his *client* was a man who would pay for quality work. Do you see what that means?" Excited, she laid her hand on the sleeve of his black pin-striped suit jacket. "The blackmailer hired someone to do his dirty work for him. It all but proves it's someone you *know*, someone close who would know your habits and cases. Someone who knew you were handling the Jerome case and who could figure out a way to get the necessary head shots of you and Karyn Jerome. Think, Nate! Who? Who would benefit most if you *did* leave Chicago?''

''I don't know!'' Nate snapped back, tired of the whole thing. ''Pick someone. How about Albert? Or what about Agnes? She's been threatening me for one thing or another for years.''

''Very funny. We've already established the fact that the blackmailer is a—Nate! That's a red light!''

He hit his brakes and barely missed broadsiding a city bus. Horns blared all around them. Swearing, Nate made a sharp right and at the first opportunity pulled over to the side of the street.

For a moment he and Rennie just sat there staring straight ahead. God, he thought, he was losing his mind. He could have killed them both. ''I'm sorry,'' he said, pinching the bridge of his nose.

Rennie waved off the apology. She understood. This arrangement was no longer working for them. There was simply too much tension. ''I think we should discuss your turning this case over to someone else,'' she said quietly. ''You have enough to go to the police now.''

''Do you want out?'' he demanded stiffly.

She turned to look out the side window. "Nate—I don't know. But it would probably be the smartest move."

"It wouldn't stop me from wanting you." He turned his head to see her shut her eyes and sighed. "I guess that answers my next question."

"Don't. Look, we need to talk."

She was offering him more than he dared hope for. "When?"

"I don't know. I have to work another case tonight and I won't be in until late."

"It doesn't matter; I have a feeling I'll be awake anyway."

Realizing it would do no good to argue with him, she reached for the door handle. "All right, then. I'll see you later."

"Wait a minute! Where are you going? We're blocks away from the office."

But she needed some time alone. "I'm parked near here."

"Rennie!"

Before he could say more she hopped out of the car and slammed the door. She had to cringe against the blast of cold air that greeted her. "That's what you get for fibbing, Paris," she muttered under her breath. Her coat was in her car, and *it* was parked on the other side of the river—in front of her apartment.

Turning up the lapels on her blazer, she hurried down the street and ducked into a pedestrian causeway to get out of the wind. She would give him two minutes, she decided, checking her watch. Then she would grab a cab back to her place and open a can of chicken soup. It didn't slip by her that catching pneumonia sounded like the only viable escape from her problems at this point.

Why did it seem that the more headway she was making in this case, the more complicated her personal life became?

It was nearly one in the morning when she passed the night security guard in the lobby of Nate's building and stepped into the elevator. Her feet were so sore from wearing her spiked heels and she was so tired, that she didn't even chuckle over the way Gus had dropped SpaghettiOs onto his tie when he saw her. She simply punched the button on Nate's floor, and slumped against the back of the car.

It was probably too much to expect Nate to have given up on her and gone to bed, but she hoped anyway. Despite what she'd agreed to before, she wasn't in any mood to talk. All she wanted to do was kick off her shoes and drop into bed, fur jacket, leather miniskirt and all.

As the elevator doors slid open at her floor, she sneezed. Great, she thought. If she wasn't taking rabbit hair out of her mouth, she was sneezing her brains out. Well, what did she expect walking around at night wearing little more than a navel warmer?

"I'm getting too old for this," she muttered, digging her keys from her purse as she headed for Nate's apartment.

As she was sliding the key into the lock she heard a crash from inside. Her reaction was quick. She reached for the automatic in her purse, locked a bullet in the chamber and burst through the door.

"Freeze!" she shouted.

Nate was on one knee picking up a lamp from the carpet. She held her crouched stance a moment longer, before easing the hammer back down and straightening.

He was alone.

She felt like a fool.

"I—I heard the crash and thought you were in trouble." Seeing the expression on his face, she quickly put her gun back into her purse.

Nate was stunned, though he told himself it was foolish to be; he knew she carried a gun— she often made jokes about it as she had at the car wash. But he'd never seen it, never thought of her having to actually use it.

And he'd never seen her dressed like that, either.

"I bumped into the table," he said, his gaze lingering on the length of leg exposed by the leather miniskirt. Questions raced through his mind. Jealousy heated his temper. "Are you trying a new approach to nabbing your Michelangelo, or is that the current look for upwardly mobile career women?"

She'd closed and locked the door and was beginning to unbuckle her shoes, but paused to shoot him a speaking glance. "I told you this afternoon that I had to work another case tonight."

"Looks like it was a lot more interesting than this one."

She watched him set the lamp back onto the side table before completing the task of undoing the straps on her shoes and slipping them off. Her movements were deft, but inside she was already bracing herself against a resurgence of nerves.

"What's wrong? Did something happen tonight? This afternoon?" she asked cautiously.

"Relax. You didn't miss any excitement."

The terse reply made her sigh inwardly. Excitement. Is that what he thought she was in this business for? She slid out of her jacket, saw his eyes narrow as her pink angora sweater slid off one shoulder, and felt her own tension rise a notch higher. "I'm not in this business for thrills." She hung the jacket on the brass coat tree. "I'm in it because I want to help people. Now, I really *am* tired, and it hasn't been the best of days...."

"I can't imagine why not. Dressed like that

you should have been inundated with propositions from men wanting your help.''

Sixteen hours on her feet and she had to listen to this? ''Who do you think you are to speak to me that way? I'll remind you that we have a business agreement between us, and that's all.''

''The hell it is,'' Nate muttered, heading toward her. As he neared, she picked up her shoes, holding them to her chest as if they were some shield to keep him away.

They didn't. Nothing could at this point.

He gripped her upper arms and gave her a single shake. ''What is this, some kind of game with you? Are you trying to see how crazy you can drive me? Well, congratulations, you've hit the jackpot!''

He locked his mouth to hers and sought a release to all the pent-up emotions he'd been storing for hours, days. At first, she fought him, pushed against his chest, tried to twist her head free. But his hold was strong, his kiss stirring.

''I've been wearing a path into this carpet worrying that something had happened to you,'' he whispered, grazing her jawline with his lips.

''I can take care of myself.'' Her breath caught as he began tracing a line down the column of her throat. ''I have been for years, and I prefer it that way.''

''Save that tough-guy act for somebody who believes it.'' He began to work his way back up her throat. "You don't prefer it, you're just scared of trying anything else. But you want to. You want *me*."

"Right now I think I hate you."

Feeling something rip his heart, he smiled bitterly. "Whatever works."

Without giving her a chance to reply or react he lifted her into his arms and carried her to the couch. Shock momentarily rendered Rennie speechless, but as she felt the soft cushions under her and Nate easing a place for himself beside her, she felt her pulse accelerate, grow uneven.

"Wait a minute." She braced her hands against his shoulders and felt power beneath the softness of his navy V-necked sweater. "You can't—"

"I already have," he replied, lowering his head to taste the exposed slope of her shoulder. Angora brushed against his cheek, but its softness was nothing compared to her skin. Wanting to explore more, he brushed his lips back and forth along her collarbone and then along the sensitive column of her throat.

"Nate, I don't want this."

"You're lying."

"But we agreed—"

"To nothing," he muttered as he pressed his open mouth to hers and kissed her with all the longing that was burning inside him.

Their tongues replaced the fencing of words.

She resisted. He dominated. He'd never forced his attentions on a woman before and he couldn't be cruel to Rennie, but her stubborn resistance was killing him.

"Kiss me back," he whispered hoarsely before teasing her lips with gentle bites. With slow deliberation, he ran his fingers across her cheek and down her throat. "Already so warm," he murmured, continuing the exploration down the length of her arm and up her ribs. "Are you burning up all over, sweetheart? Let me see."

He traced the underside of her breast and Rennie felt fingers of flames lick at her hardening nipple. She closed her eyes, wanting to deny it felt good, but when he covered her completely with his hand, she couldn't contain her whimper of pleasure.

Panic seized her. She had to stop him before it was too late. This couldn't happen, she thought, beginning to shake her head. She couldn't give that much of herself again. She wouldn't.

"Please stop," she whispered. But Nate continued to caress her through her sweater while nuzzling her ear. Her spine ready to snap from its rigidity, she gripped his wrist. "Nate—damn it, if you're my friend, *don't*!"

He went still, raised his head and looked down at her. There was no mistaking the anguish in her eyes and, suddenly, he closed his and buried his face in her fragrant hair. "God. I didn't mean to—I mean, I wouldn't have—"

She winced hearing the torment in his voice and lifted her hand to stroke his hair. "I know. It's not your fault. It's mine."

His reply was explicit. He raised his head to give her an exasperated look. "How do you figure that?"

She couldn't meet his intent gaze. It was hard enough to lie there quietly while feeling their bodies fused together from breast to thigh. "Because I suppose I was giving off signals even though I was trying not to and you read me too well. I won't lie to you any longer, Nate. I do want you. But it can't go any further than that."

He stared at the picture she made with her hair fanning out around her and felt hurt slice through him. "Why?"

"I—I'm just not any good at casual sex."

"What makes you think it would be casual?"

She thought about Madeline but decided against using her as a defense. "I'm not capable of anything more." She uttered a short, bitter laugh. "Apparently I'm not even capable of that."

What was she trying to tell him? "Are you saying you think you're frigid?"

"No." As she remembered that one, all-too-short kiss in the parking garage that weekend, as well as her response a few moments ago, embarrassment sent a surge of heat to her face. "But I decided a long time ago that I wasn't very successful in that department and that I could lead a contented life without it, without any deep relationship."

Nate studied her a moment longer before sitting up. "I think it's time for that talk you mentioned earlier."

He shifted to sit in one corner of the sofa. As Rennie tried to use the opportunity to put some distance between them, he slipped his arm around her waist and drew her back against him.

"Uh-uh," he said, settling her between his legs. "You're staying here."

The arrangement was, in its own way, no less intimate than the other. Feeling his heart thudding against her back and her hips cradled by his, she closed her eyes. "Why are you being difficult?"

Nate planted a kiss near her temple. "I thought I was supposed to be a friend."

"Friends sit at the kitchen table over cups of coffee."

"I'm not sleepy and my nerves are jumpy enough without the caffeine. So are yours," he said, glancing down at the way she had her hands clasped tightly in her lap. He gently forced them apart and enclosed them within his. "There. Feel better? I feel better."

Reluctantly Rennie chuckled. "And you've

had the nerve to accuse *me* of being the crazy one?''

''You don't hate me anymore?''

''You know I never meant that. I was only—''

''Scared?''

Scared. He pulled so many emotions out of her, made her want so much. But couldn't he see? ''Nate, I have lousy luck.''

He understood her impulse to turn this into something more lighthearted, but he wasn't going to let her get away with it. ''No jokes this time. Talk to me from the heart.''

She was nothing but scar tissue there. With a sigh, she leaned her head back against his shoulder. ''Everyone I've ever cared about has either died or walked out on me. Can you understand what I'm saying?''

''You've been hurt a lot. Tell me.''

Where should she begin? It all went back to her earliest memories. ''I never knew my father. My mother said he was a musician, but I don't know... you've heard me sing.''

''Knock it off.''

''Listen,'' she began indignantly, ''I'll do this my way or you can lump it.''

Unperturbed, he played with a lock of her hair. ''I find it fascinating that whenever I make the slightest headway with you, you turn into a little toughie.''

''Well, my instincts come from the street. You

knew that Fred helped raise me, but what you don't know is that I was ten when my mother died and for the better part of the next two years, I all but lived out there on my own.''

Nate swore softly. "Wasn't there anyone...a neighbor, social services?"

"Among others," she agreed. "They tried to stick me in a foster home a couple of times. I'm not going to say they're all bad, but it's the luck-of-the-draw type of situation, you know? Boy, did I get some winners. I decided my chances were better on the streets."

His own experiences were all reinforced with love and support, but no one could live in a city like Chicago and not have a perception of the extremes that were in the life-styles of its inhabitants. "Until Fred," he murmured, silently sending a prayer of thanks to the man he'd never had a chance to meet. He rested his cheek against her head.

"Until Fred." She smiled, remembering him. "I used to sleep in his car. He was terrible about forgetting to lock it. I would crawl in there and cover myself with cardboard boxes or whatever I could find, then clear out before he went to work in the morning. Unfortunately he was real late coming home one night so I had to wait for my bed. I overslept and he caught me."

"What was it, an instant mutual admiration society?"

"Are you serious? Fred hated kids—or so he often said. But he was a real softy inside. The problem was, at twelve, I thought I knew everything. I put him through hell that first year. Finally we worked things out. He bullied me through school and then taught me the business."

"How old were you when he died?"

"Twenty-one. God, I was lost without him. He was my rock. I guess that's why when Alan came along, it didn't take much for him to sweep me off my feet."

Nate felt a rush of jealousy and forced himself to ignore it. "What did he do for a living?"

"As little as possible," she replied dryly. "Alan was gorgeous and he decided that's all he had to be. I didn't care. I was infatuated, and I was making a living keeping the agency going." She looked down at the masculine hands that were holding hers and realized suddenly that, as crazy as she'd been about him, she and her ex-husband had never shared a moment like this.

"What happened?" Nate asked gently.

"He got bored and left with another woman, taking every penny we had. I thought, well, okay, I still have the business. Then a few weeks later the husband of a client walked into my office. The big gorilla discovered that his wife had hired me to follow him. He didn't take it well. It earned me a trip to the hospital for a couple of weeks. After I got out, I decided being that accessible was for the birds and started my referral service."

"My God...I had no idea."

She lifted a shoulder dismissing the compassion she heard in his voice. "Sometimes I think I ought to sell my life story to Hollywood. I could be the female Mike Hammer. What do you think?"

"I think I owe you an apology for giving you such a hard time and pushing you as I did," he said, brushing her hair back over her shoulder and toying with her dangly rose quartz earring.

"You don't owe me anything, Nate. I just wanted you to understand why it's better for us to keep things the way they were. Your friendship means a lot to me, but I don't want to deal with anything more complicated. The emotional cost is too high."

Nate let her rise from the couch only because he knew that if he continued to hold her, he would be tempted to prove how little she knew herself. She might be afraid of getting involved again, but the needs were all there, along with the dreams. He was certain enough not to give up hoping that they included him. "What if you don't have a choice, Rennie? Sometimes no matter how hard your mind tries to control things, your heart decides not to listen."

"I think that's something poets and songwriters dreamed up," she said, collecting her shoes and purse. "Now what do you say we call it a night while we can still agree to disagree?"

"On one condition."

She watched him get up and circle around to her, felt her heart begin to pound as the low light illuminated the intent look in his dark eyes. "What?" she managed in a strained voice.

"Kiss me good-night."

She exhaled wearily. "Nate. Has nothing I said sunk in with you?"

In response he gently grasped her shoulders and touched his lips to hers. The kiss was like an angel's caress and Rennie felt a suspicious burning in the backs of her eyes, a feeling she hadn't allowed herself to experience in years. When he released her, she shook her head feeling both bemused and exasperated.

"What am I going to do with you?"

He gave her a slow wink. "Sleep on it. You'll think of something."

Chapter Six

When Rennie dragged herself into the kitchen the following morning, the last thing she expected to see was Nate standing by the coffee maker. She glanced at her watch and frowned.

"Logic tells me that you're a figment of my imagination."

He looked over his shoulder, taking in the untamed curls that contradicted the conservative intent he sensed behind her holly-green two-piece suit, without missing the shadows beneath her eyes. Easy does it, he told himself. It was only natural that she would try to reestablish perimeters this morning.

"Instinct tells me you didn't get any more sleep than I did," he replied. "Have a seat. The coffee's done but the croissants will take a minute longer to warm."

"You're supposed to be at the office." She resented his being here when she wasn't ready to face him again, and it didn't help that he looked perfect as usual in his crisp white shirt, and light gray vest and pants.

"I called and said I'd be late. I knew you needed me."

"I don't need you. I need coffee."

With an amused lift of his brows, Nate poured two mugs of the brew and carried them to the table. "Are you going to bite my head off if I mention that you look especially nice this morning?"

"I wouldn't 'bite your head off' at all if you wouldn't insist on flirting with me, even before I'm awake."

"I wasn't flirting," he replied, taking the croissants out of the oven and transferring them to the basket on the counter. He carried it to the table and sat down beside her. "I was merely making an observation. Can I help it if I like the way you look?"

"My hair is a mess and I'm not wearing any makeup yet."

"Yeah? Wait a minute." Leaning back in his chair, he tilted his head and studied her through narrowed eyes. "Hmm. You're right. Maybe you *do* look terrible. Thanks for bringing that to my attention."

"Idiot." Rennie hid her smile by taking a

careful sip of her coffee. Just what she needed this morning—a comedian. But she had to admit this was a lot more pleasant than arguing.

"Have one of these."

She watched him tear the end off one of the flaky croissants and pop it in his mouth. "No, thanks. I don't eat breakfast."

"This isn't breakfast. This is a bluff to your brain to make it *think* it's getting breakfast. Sunday I'll make you a real breakfast."

"I don't eat breakfast," she told him again. But this time she didn't bother trying to hide the laughter in her eyes.

Wanting much more, Nate turned his concentration to pouring cream into his coffee. Last night in bed he made lists instead of counting sheep. On one list he itemized all the reasons he shouldn't be having the thoughts he'd been having about her. There were the obvious items on top, like the fact that she wasn't interested in getting involved, and that she would need a lot of tender caring to heal the emotional damage she'd suffered—and even then there were no guarantees—all the way down to the small matter of her not being particularly cheerful in the morning.

Then he listed all the reasons why he *should* be having those thoughts, starting with the fact that he liked to look at her and touch her, he liked the way her hair smelled and the way she talked to herself when she thought she was alone. But the most interesting thing was that everything on the other list started showing up on this one. She might not want to get involved, but he could tell by her eyes that she at least thought about getting involved with *him*. She needed tender caring, and he wanted to be the one who supplied it. She wasn't a morning person, but already there was laughter in her lovely eyes.

Finally he'd put aside his lists and let the realization come like a soft down blanket spreading over him on a cold, lonely night. He was falling in love. It was the last thing he remembered thinking before he drifted off to sleep. Now it made him feel full and warm and generous—generous enough to give her the time and space she needed to get used to him.

"So what's on your agenda for today?" he asked.

Her smile faded as she remembered a phone call she had to make. She stared at the thriving ivy plant in the center of the table and wondered again if it would be wrong to lie in order not to shatter hope?

"Did I say something wrong?"

"No. I'm thinking about how I could ease the disappointment of an old man, but I'm afraid it's impossible. I've been looking for his teenage granddaughter," she explained, seeing his confusion. "The only problem is, she doesn't want to be found."

"Is that what you were doing last night?" When she nodded, he grimaced, remembering what he'd thought when he saw her and the things he'd suggested.

"Forget it. You couldn't know."

"You must have been tempted to knock my teeth in."

"Lucky for you I have great willpower."

"I'll say. Come here." Without giving her a chance to comply or refuse, he drew her out of her chair and onto his lap.

"Nate, I thought we agreed?"

"Uh-uh. All I remember is that you talked and I listened. Now don't complicate this. I just wanted to give you a hug, okay? Pal to pal. And you don't always have to work at being strong around me," he added, giving her another gentle squeeze. "I'm not going to think you're any less of a professional if you act human once in a while."

Rennie resisted the ache a moment longer before giving in to the need to wrap her arms around his neck. With a sigh, she closed her eyes and let the rush of emotion come, leaving a lump in her throat. "You know, I really can't stand you when you're nice like this."

"Thanks. I think you're a real pain, too." He forced himself to keep the kiss he gave her undemanding and not to resist when she moved back to her own chair. "Does this mean you'll let me buy you lunch today?"

"Can't," she said, feeling a bit off balance and bemused. If she was more of a romantic, she would swear she'd just been sprinkled with fairy dust. "I'm meeting Faith Dillard, remember?"

He made a disparaging sound while breaking off another piece of croissant. "Refresh my memory. What do you hope to accomplish by talking to her?"

"I'll let you know once I've decided." She picked up her mug and rose from the table.

"Where are you going?"

"To finish getting ready."

"But—" The phone rang cutting him off. He reached for the cordless phone on the counter behind him and, a moment after answering, gestured to her. "Lady Macbeth," he whispered, covering the mouthpiece with his hand.

Rennie lightly pinched his arm before accepting the receiver. "Good morning, Faith. What's up?"

"I, um, I'm sorry if I bothered you. I thought Nate would have left for the office by now."

"That makes two of us, but he's being a pest this morning." She spun out of reach as he made a playful grab for her. "Is something wrong?"

"You're going to think I'm making this up, but I have to cancel our lunch plans. Wendell called me this morning. He said Maggie wasn't feeling well and asked me to take her place at her ladies' club luncheon today. It has to be serious; she's supposed to receive a community service award and she wouldn't want to miss something like that. How could I say no?''

''I understand perfectly. It looks like we'll just make it Thursday after all.''

''No, I'm afraid not. There's something else. Albert surprised me with an offer to go out of town with him for a long weekend. You know I'm not about to turn down an offer like that.''

''I don't blame you. Well, then call me when you get back, and tell Maggie I hope she's feeling better soon.''

Nate watched her as she replaced the phone in its cradle and reached for her coffee mug. ''What's that perplexed frown for?'' he asked, running a finger along one of the folds of her full skirt.

''I'm not sure. Did you know that Albert was taking a long weekend?''

''No. Wait a minute. Wendell was looking for someone to represent the firm at some function in St. Louis, but I didn't know he'd asked Albert.''

''Apparently he has, and Faith is going with him. She's also canceling our lunch date because she's filling in for Maggie at an awards luncheon.''

''I gather Maggie's feeling under the weather?

Too bad." But it opened a golden opportunity for him. "Does that mean you're free to have lunch with me?"

"No," she replied, refilling her mug and heading for her room. "That means I have more time to follow other leads for your case."

Twenty minutes later they stepped from the elevator and headed for their cars. Rennie thought Nate would have left for work by now, but he seemed determined to wait for her.

"Will you at least call me and let me know where you are, how you're doing?" he asked, as she dug her keys out of her raincoat pocket.

"You know how I feel about talking on the phone."

"We can devise a code. You can say something like, 'I miss you, darling,' and I'll know you're all right. Or you can say you can't wait for me to get home and I'll know you found something."

She imagined herself calling him "darling" now and her tongue got stuck on the roof of her mouth. It was, she decided, one thing to assume a character when you were simply working a case, and entirely another when you were covering your own complex feelings. Everything was getting so mixed up.

"A code, huh?" she drawled. "All right. How about if I say something like 'Would you pick up a dozen eggs on your way home?' and that'll mean—Nate!''

He playfully grabbed her from behind. At least it started out as playful. But then he breathed in that fresh scent that was hers alone and suddenly the teasing became a wanting, sharp and insistent. He was so absorbed in her he missed her going still in his arms.

"Nate, look!"

Their cars were parked side by side and she was staring into his. Warily he stepped around her and looked through the passenger's window. It was then that he saw the small package in the driver's seat. Shock and disbelief came quickly, and with it a sense of déjà vu. Not another one, he thought. Just as before, the car had been locked. He reached for his keys.

"No!" Realizing what he meant to do, Rennie pulled his arm. "It could be a trap."

"What do you mean a—" He froze, comprehension coming quickly. A bomb.

He spun around and stared at Rennie, seeing her concern for him mirrored in her eyes, and understanding in that fragment of time what had suddenly become too precious to risk losing. He *wouldn't* lose her, he vowed, taking her arm.

"Where are we going?"

"Back upstairs," he said grimly. "It's time I called the police."

The bleary-eyed detective left the two men from the police bomb-squad unit and walked across the garage to where Rennie and Nate stood waiting. "You know you should have called us when this whole thing first began," he told Rennie.

"The decision to handle this privately was mine, Detective Killian," Nate replied before she could respond. "If you have a complaint, tell me."

As the other man gave Nate a speculative look, Rennie asked, "What could you have done other than patrol the garages more often and maybe put a wiretap on his phone—which would have proved fruitless, since he hasn't received any threatening calls?"

With deceptive indifference, Jim Killian reached into his pocket and pulled out a packet of gum. After offering a stick to each of them, he unwrapped one for himself. "I met Fred Paris a couple of times," he said conversationally, as if she hadn't spoken. "Respected him—even though he had a tendency not to call us, either."

One of the men shouted from across the garage. Killian glanced over and sighed.

"They can't see any tampering so they're going to open the car now. Are you sure I can't get you to go wait upstairs?"

Nate glanced at the two men, strangers who

were willing to risk their own lives for his safety, and shook his head. But he turned to Rennie.

"Don't even think it," she muttered. She turned to the middle-aged detective. "Let's get this over with."

He nodded to the man waiting for his signal. An instant later there was a muffled explosion. Someone yelled to get down, someone swore. Rennie felt arms going around her even as she ducked behind the last car in the aisle. She didn't have to look to know it was Nate. They barely had time to do more when one of the bomb squad members shouted to them.

"Killian, you're buying tonight! It's only a smoke bomb."

He rubbed his dark, whiskered jaw. "Nerveless little Sicilian," he muttered under his breath. After maneuvering himself to his feet, he headed for the Mercedes while Rennie and Nate brushed off their clothes.

Smoke was pouring out of the sedan and spreading throughout the garage. "You're going to have one heck of a cleaning and fumigating bill," she told Nate. "And if I were you, I'd seriously consider putting in a burglar alarm system."

Killian returned with a sheet of paper. "Someone chose an interesting way to send you a love letter."

Nate accepted the note without comment. It

was made with cutout letters just like the other one had been. Beside him, Rennie leaned closer to read it as well.

Last chance. You'd better take me seriously.

She was unaware that her grip on his arm had tightened, but Nate felt it and shifted to move his arm protectively around her waist. He met Killian's enigmatic look and let him know that, while he couldn't stop him from thinking what he would, he'd better not hear any of those assumptions vocalized.

The veteran cop tugged at his left earlobe and turned to view the progress of the two uniformed police over by the Mercedes. "It looks like they're going to be a while. Why don't we go back upstairs and you can show me the rest of the goodies. By the way, it wouldn't hurt to have an alarm system put in that thing."

Nate saw Rennie lower her head and knew she was hiding a grin. "Would it have stopped him from getting in?"

"No, but if someone heard the alarm, they might have had a chance to see the guy and we might have some kind of a description."

"Approximately six feet tall, one hundred seventy pounds with black slicked-back hair," Rennie said, reciting what she'd wheedled out of the photographer.

Killian compressed his lips together and shoved his hands deep into the pockets of his all-weather coat. For several seconds he stared at the cement floor.

"I was going to tell you."

"When? The day before they award me my gold watch? You're beginning to sound more and more like the Paris I used to know."

"Thanks."

"It wasn't— Never mind. Are you going to tell me *how* you got this information?"

"As long as you don't ask me who gave me the tip."

He rubbed his stomach, wincing. "My doctor told me I shouldn't get excited so I'm going to pretend you didn't say that. Let's go upstairs."

Fifteen minutes later, the three of them were sitting in Nate's living room. Killian gulped down the rest of his coffee and set the mug on the coffee table, while Nate finished his call to Agnes.

"Is everything all right?" Rennie asked, wishing she could offer some kind of comfort. She could see the effect all this was beginning to have on him and she didn't know how much longer he would tolerate sitting back and doing nothing. He wasn't the type of man to let others handle his problems.

Nate shot her an intimate, reassuring look. He'd missed two meetings and a judge was threatening to cite him with contempt of court, but he wasn't going to trouble her with that. It

seemed the least he could do when she seemed
to be single-handedly fighting to keep some kind
of sane balance in his life.

Rennie turned back to Jim Killian. "Well, now
you know everything we know."

"This is quite a scheme you two have dreamed
up," the police detective said, closing his notebook. "But what worries me is how much of this
arrangement is cover and how much is real?"

Nate began to rise. "You're out of line, Killian."

"Nate, it's all right."

"Easy," the older man said, holding up his
hand. "Try to remember that I'm on your side,
okay? All I'm saying is that it's clear you care
about the lady and she cares about you. And
while I have to admit she's done a decent job so
far...though I'd still like to know how she ob-
tained some of her information—" he shot Rennie a sour look "—the question that comes to *my*
mind is, are you still willing to let her operate in
the same capacity as she has been? This is a risky
situation and you don't know what kind of tiger
you're trying to grab by the tail here. Are you
going to be able to live with yourself if something happens to her? Now, what I'd like to suggest is that we put you under our own surveil-
lance."

"That's unacceptable," Rennie said, barely
suppressing her anger. "I've already told you

that whoever's behind this is a person who's either professionally or personally close to Nate. Your people would stick out like snowmen on the Fourth of July! All the blackmailer will have to do is keep a low profile until you give up. And don't forget his courier—he's already proven he's sharper than we anticipated.''

"It's a risk that might be worth taking," Nate said quietly.

Rennie jerked her head around to give him an incredulous look. "You can't mean that? Don't you see what he's doing? He's just trying to squeeze me off this case."

Killian glanced from one of them to the other and, dropping a business card on the coffee table, slowly rose to his feet. "I think this is where I discreetly excuse myself. Talk it over and give me a call."

As the door closed behind him, Rennie rose and went to the sliding glass doors. It was midmorning and the sun reflected brilliantly on the lake. In the distance a freighter was making its way to port. Was it coming home, or was it flying a foreign flag? What marvelous things ships were. They could put men on the moon and negotiate billions of dollars' worth of contracts over a few bits of wire, but ships were still necessary. They still got the job done. On the other hand, people were replaceable; *she* was replaceable.

"Funny how people get this time of year, isn't

it?'' she said, rubbing her hands up and down her arms. ''The first sign of cool weather and the mention of the holidays, and suddenly it's all peace on earth and goodwill toward everyone. I suppose the extra patrolling in the garage won't hurt. And about the alarm system—I could take you to the office and then—''

His hands gripped her shoulders. She hadn't heard him coming, and she gave a start, more for the incredible tenderness in his touch than his surprising her.

''Rennie, it's something we have to face.''

She gave an awkward laugh and, shrugging off his hands, went to retrieve Killian's empty coffee mug. ''Really, there's nothing to it,'' she said, purposely misunderstanding him. ''I drop you off and take the car to get it cleaned up, then have the system put in.''

''You know what I was talking about; I was referring to *us*. I want you off the case.''

Rennie carried the mug to the sink and stood there a moment. *I know this feeling,* she thought. It was the same one she'd experienced when she heard Fred's heart monitor go berserk, the same one she felt when she came home one night with Alan's favorite Chinese take-out only to find him and all his things gone. It was an absolute hollowness.

She laced and unlaced her fingers and slowly

returned to the living room. "Why?" she demanded flatly.

"Because he was right."

"He was pushing buttons, Nate. He's annoyed that he wasn't called in sooner and he's using whatever means necessary to get you to cooperate with him. But I'm the professional you hired and I intend to see this case through to its completion."

"The decision isn't yours to make."

He'd been standing as she had before, staring out at the lake, but as he turned, something cold gripped her heart. His face was a terrible mask, no less handsome, but frozen in its resolution.

"You can't mean this," she whispered. "I have time invested in this case. Even more, it's a matter of principle."

"Do you think I care about principle when it comes to your *life*? We're starting a relationship here, Rennie."

"Stop it!" She closed her hands over her ears. "We're only friends!"

Nate covered the small distance between them and grabbed her wrists, giving her an impatient shake. "Yes, we're friends, Rennie. But we're *going* to be lovers. It's inevitable."

"Thanks for the offer, but I'm not interested in filling in while you and Madeline iron out your differences."

He let her go, his expression confused. "What are you talking about? I told you that was over."

"Is that why you took the first opportunity you found the other night to cross the room to talk to her?"

"I told you she has problems."

"Don't we all?"

"Rennie, for heaven's sake, she's been playing around with cocaine!"

Shocked, she watched him turn away from her and rake his hands through his hair. Whatever she'd expected, it wasn't this. Madeline seemed to have everything—looks, money. Why? What was the attraction? "I'm sorry," she said hesitantly. "I'm sure it must have been a painful discovery for you."

"We were already having problems, it just compounded them." He swung back to her. "But it still doesn't have anything to do with this and what's between us."

Rennie closed her eyes. "Nate, please. All I want is to be able to do my job and move on to the next one. Whatever this chemistry is between us, it'll pass once we're back to leading our normal lives."

"Will it?" He stepped closer and slowly framed her face with his hands. Unlike his heart, his hands were steady. "How can you be so certain? Do you really think you can move out of here and forget this?" He touched his lips to hers. "And this?" he whispered, teasing her senses by deepening the kiss and flicking his tongue against hers.

"It's what I want. It's what I've decided is best for me."

"I don't believe you."

Needing to prove her wrong, he took her mouth again, but this time his kiss wasn't the tender coaxing as before. This time there was temper and determination. It was the only thing that made it possible for Rennie to stand there and not fight him.

And yet, even angry, Nate was a charismatic man. Strong. Exciting. With that first kiss alone, he left her senses sizzling. Then he slid his fingers deep into her hair and sought to burn down her defenses one by one.

Discipline. He felt it in her as she steeled herself against his ardent assault. It hurt him as much as it fueled his own determination. Didn't she understand? It wasn't just the physical attraction. But it started here, with this passion, with this need he had for her to acknowledge that on at least one level they were irrevocably connected.

She felt as if her lifeblood was being drained from her and she was losing everything—emotion, thought, willpower. Would he leave her empty? she wondered, feeling the trembling again. Was this to be her punishment for resisting him? A future of remembering the man who wouldn't be ignored? Dear God, what had made her think she could walk away from him with her sanity intact?

It was her broken sob that made him draw back. He raised his head and stared transfixed at her pale face. Her eyes were closed, her lashes dry, but he could swear she was a heartbeat away from tears. Impulsively he touched her cheek. He hadn't meant to hurt her.

"Rennie—"

"Damn you," she whispered, glaring at him through eyes that were so blurred with tears they were as useless as the bits of pretty glass falling out of a shattered kaleidoscope. "Why couldn't you have left it alone? Did you have to ruin *everything*?"

She ran blindly to the door, barely remembering to grab her purse. She didn't hear him call after her. She didn't hear the apartment door slam as she pulled it closed behind her. All she knew was the pain—and hadn't she promised herself never to let anyone hurt her again?

Chapter Seven

"Can I walk her now?"

Rennie hesitated only slightly before smiling at the little girl with the missing front tooth and handing her the blue suede leash. "Just once more around the swing sets, Narissa, and then I'm going to have to take her home."

The sun was still reasonably high, but Rennie wanted to get back to her apartment. It had been only guilt that made her bring Arabella to the park for a walk in the first place. She would have preferred being alone right now, curled into a tight knot and feeling sorry for herself. She didn't want to have to put on this bright smile for Narissa and the other children who'd come over to pet and play with her cat. But she'd grown tired of listening to Belle's incessant complaining about being housebound for the past several days.

As the child led the regal Persian away, Rennie sat on a wooden bench to wait. The wind whipped her skirt and hair and made her shiver. However, she knew she could be in her apartment, curled up under a pile of blankets right now, and she would still be shivering, because her condition had less to do with the weather than with her state of mind.

The day had gone from bad to terrible. After leaving Nate, she'd regained her composure and reported to her other client. It was a mistake, or maybe being too honest about the probability of his granddaughter returning had been a mistake. At any rate, he'd become upset, too, and now she was minus a second client. If this was a trend, she thought gloomily, she was going to be forced to advertise soon.

She shivered again and her thoughts involuntarily returned to Nate. Was he at the office now? Did he manage to get the car to a shop all right? At his condominium, she'd left the warmer on under the coffeepot; did he remember to shut it off? Was he thinking of her? She closed her eyes, accepting the pain and the regret, just as she accepted that the taste of his kisses still lingered on her lips.

How quickly life became complicated. She'd worked at keeping things simple for so long, yet in a matter of days she'd managed not only to make a mess out of her professional life but her private life as well. Maybe she needed a vacation. Wouldn't that be a first? She'd never had the inclination to take one before. It might be nice to pack up Belle and go away somewhere. But where would she go that her memories wouldn't follow? And how could she go anywhere while knowing that Nate might be in danger?

A heavy hand gripped her shoulder from behind, causing her heart—her whole body—to jolt. She tightened her grip on her purse, ready to use it as a weapon. Come on, she thought, ready for a good fight. She spun around.

It was only Rocco.

"He wants to see you," the unsmiling giant grumbled.

She slumped back against the bench, annoyance quickly replacing relief. "Are you crazy, sneaking up on me like that?"

"He wants to see you."

Leave it to Rocco not to mince words, she thought, gritting her teeth. She glanced around him and almost groaned when she saw the black stretch limousine waiting by the curb. So much for her attempts at keeping a low profile in this neighborhood.

When she turned back around, Narissa stood before her, clutching Belle close to her chest. "You'd better let me have her, sweetheart," she said, taking the cat out of her arms. "There

seems to be this appointment that I have to go
to.''

''My mommy says you're not supposed to talk
to strange men or get in their cars.'' She pointed
at Rocco. ''He looks like a bad man.''

Rocco transferred his unfriendly gaze to the
child. ''Beat it, kid.''

Narissa's mouth fell open a second before she
ran off wailing. Rennie took a moment to adjust
her hold on Belle before shooting DePalma's
bodyguard a weary look.

''Tactful, Rocco. Really tactful.''

She circled him and walked over to the limousine. The door opened and Mario DePalma
peered out to give her a much warmer greeting.

''You're a difficult woman to locate today.
Come in. We'll go for a drive.''

Without waiting for her to reply, he shifted
over. Now what? she wondered as she climbed
in. Rocco shut the door behind her and took his
seat beside the chauffeur, who was no light-
weight, either. The car eased away from the curb
as though floating on air.

''I hope you don't mind my bringing along a
friend?'' she drawled, taking off her sunglasses
and giving Arabella a reassuring scratch under
her chin.

''Any friend of yours, Rennie...you know
that.'' But when he reached across the seat, it
wasn't to stroke the cat; he cupped Rennie's chin

in his hand and turned it toward him so that he could freely study her face. "You've had a hard day."

"I'll bet you're dynamite with tea leaves."

"I'm better with telephones and informants. You want me to lie and tell you that I hadn't heard about that unfortunate incident this morning?"

Her answering smile was cynical. "Which one?"

"Only the one that was any of my business, my dear." He gave her cheek an affectionate pat before removing his hand. "You know I'm not the type to meddle in things that don't concern me."

Rennie dropped her head back against the plush leather seat and gave in to the chuckle that bubbled up her throat. "Heaven help me, but I like you."

"As long as you can still laugh, I suppose I shouldn't be too offended by the idea of being the brunt of your humor. Tell me then, have the police any leads yet?"

"I wouldn't know; I've been officially removed from the case."

DePalma rattled off a stream of Italian that left Rennie wondering whether she'd been blessed, or Nate condemned to a life of bad wine and worse food. Even the chauffeur gave him a cautious glance in the rearview mirror.

"You almost solve this case for him and he fires you?"

"You give me too much credit. How far would I be, if it wasn't for your strong leads?"

"God gives the seed for the grape, Rennie. But it takes the right touch, and much labor to make the seed grow and yield fruit."

"Is that why you insisted Rocco accompany me to that photographer?" she asked innocently.

DePalma adjusted the topcoat draped over his shoulders. "The analogy works only so far, Rennie. The fact remains I'm displeased by what your Mr. Montgomery has done to you. I'm tempted to tell my attorneys that when they go to that meeting tomorrow—"

"Positively not. Nate has enough problems right now, he doesn't need the added worry of the Jerome negotiations falling apart. And he's not *my* Mr. Montgomery."

"Yet you defend him?"

She concentrated on adjusting Belle's collar. "He only fired me because he thought it was a way to protect me."

"*Ahh.*"

Rennie shot him a warning look. "Whatever you're thinking, don't. I told you there's nothing between us."

"Whatever you say."

"I'd have been satisfied being left alone to do my job," she muttered mostly to herself.

"Of course."

"If I had an ounce of sense, I'd leave him to the police and forget about him."

"Is that what you've decided to do?"

"How can I?" she cried. "Every instinct in me says that this blackmailing is getting out of hand. I don't know how to explain it, but I have a terrible feeling that Nate's in some real physical danger."

DePalma nodded. "I agree; it's the other reason why I'm here. Does the name Tilman mean anything to you?"

"I don't think so."

"He's small-time, an unsavory individual. I think this Tilman is the man you're looking for." As Rennie began to speak, he held up his hand. "No, I don't have proof or details. I hear whispers from the street. They say this man is bragging about having a contract to do something he would have done for free. Equally important is that he matches the description of the man the photographer spoke of."

Rennie looked out the tinted side window, but she saw nothing of the neighborhood they were passing through. Her mind's eye was focused on Nate and she was wondering how she was going to help him when he didn't want her near him. She could pass this information on to the police; she could even call Nate and warn him about this new development...but would it be enough?

"Where can I find this Tilman?"

DePalma shrugged, his expression turning apologetic. "He's gone underground. No one has seen him in two, maybe three days."

The quiet before the storm. It was a cliché, but one that she believed. All right, she thought, she could keep an eye on Nate's condominium and the office without the police even being aware of it. But how was she going to stay near him when he went out?

"Oh, God. There's the mayor's ball tomorrow night. We were supposed to go." Under the circumstances would he be tempted to stay home?

"Not likely," DePalma replied, though she wasn't aware she'd voiced the question out loud. "More deals are struck and contacts made at that event than at half the year's business lunches."

"Don't feel obligated to cheer me up. I'm already aware of the fact that I can't get in there without his taking me."

"You can go with me." Her stunned expression made him laugh outright. "It surprises you that the Chairman of the Board and Chief Executive Officer of Morgan Towers should be rubbing elbows with the mayor and other members of the city's elite?"

"Ah—no, of course not. But I'm sure you made other arrangements for the evening."

"I'm a generous patron of the mayor's favorite community projects; I'm sure I won't be denied bringing along one more guest. And once we're there, I would think it only a matter of time before Mr. Montgomery notices you and claims your attentions for himself.''

"Probably to read me the riot act." He would be furious, especially when he discovered she'd sneaked back into the condominium to get the gown she'd planned to wear to the event. But even as she worried, she knew it would be worth it.

She nodded her head decisively. "All right, I'd be delighted to accompany you to the ball.''

"Good…and once Montgomery sees you, he'll forget everything except that he's happy to have you there. Wait. You will see that I am right.''

Rennie managed a vague smile. She would settle for him just not creating a scene.

Nate stood beside Wendell and Maggie Dillard as they chatted with the mayor, but he heard only bits and pieces of their conversation. He didn't know if he had an opinion on whether the city should attempt an artistic exchange program with some third-world countries or not; at this point he couldn't even be sure why he'd come tonight. He certainly didn't *want* to be here. Only the thought of the firm's responsibility to the community and the image his absence would project to others finally convinced him to drag out his formal wear and put in an appearance. But now, after being here less than an hour, he was already counting the minutes until he could make his excuses and leave.

He was miserable, and it was all Rennie's fault. For the second day in a row, he'd failed in his attempts to contact her. He'd left a dozen messages with her answering service, but she hadn't returned any of his calls.

In a way he couldn't blame her; maybe he *had* pushed too hard yesterday when he'd asked her to accept something that she was obviously not ready to face. Maybe he should have given her more time before he'd started talking about relationships and getting serious. But having discovered a treasure of feelings for her, he'd become greedy—or could wanting to experience everything there was to experience with her be construed as a form of generosity? He wished he believed it were true. It might make him feel less of a heel when he remembered the look she'd had on her face when she ran out on him.

Why did you have to ruin everything?

God, that had been cruel. Why hadn't she just taken a knife and stabbed him through the heart?

On the other hand, there was something he could be grateful for. He was glad that she was out of this mess. Killian seemed to have things under control. He'd kept his word and patrol cars were cruising the garages regularly; the security people in both buildings had been put on alert; and protection outside the country club was heavy. He couldn't imagine anyone trying anything. As Killian mentioned, half of the top brass of the police department and judicial system were in attendance tonight. The only place he would be safer was in a private cell at the city jail.

But where he wanted to be was home, nursing his bruised feelings—not to mention making plans for what to do once this mess was over in order to convince Rennie that there was no way he was going to disappear from her life.

"Nate? What do you think of the Bears' chances of making the Super Bowl this year?"

He couldn't care less. "Excuse me, won't you?" He indicated his near-empty glass. "I could use a refill."

As he walked away, he heard Wendell discreetly apologizing for him, mentioning the strain of a considerable caseload. He twisted his lips into a bitter smile, wondering why Wendell didn't just acknowledge that he was depressed because Rennie had walked out on him. Hadn't enough people already noticed she wasn't with him tonight?

"Bourbon and water," he said upon arriving at the makeshift bar. As he waited, he slipped his hands into his pants pockets and turned around to see the steady stream of people still arriving. It wouldn't be long before the main ballroom was packed. Then he would be able to slip away without even Wendell noticing his absence.

"Bourbon and water, sir."

"Thanks." He slipped a bill into the bartender's tip jar, and turning, raised his drink to his lips. A moment later bourbon lodged in his throat.

Rennie! Good God—and was that DePalma she was with?

A waiter passed carrying a tray of champagne. Nate added his glass to it and began to weave his way through the crowd toward them. Of all the insane stunts, he fumed. Suddenly melancholia turned into red-hot anger.

But even furious he didn't miss that she looked stunning. Her gown was like liquid bronze shimmering from her throat to her ankles, and familiar. Wasn't that the one he'd seen her hanging up the day she moved in? he asked himself. How did she get it? She hadn't— But knowing Rennie, she obviously had.

Rennie saw only fury when she spotted him. For an instant she felt the strongest urge to turn and run. Then she reminded herself of the compact she'd stumbled upon in the living room when she'd gone to pick up her dress, and it gave her the courage to lift her chin and meet his fierce glare calmly. He'd better not say a word, she told herself. He wanted a relationship with her, her foot! The moment she left, he must have been on the phone inviting Madeline back into his bed. Well, she would show him. She was here to finish her job and that was that.

Mario DePalma spotted Nate, too, and placed a hand at the small of her back telegraphing his reassurance. "Just the man I was going to look for," he said, as Nate reached them. "Look who I discovered stranded and in need of a ride."

"Why didn't you simply call and tell me, *sweetheart*?" Nate murmured, taking a firm grip of Rennie's wrist. Without giving her a chance to reply, he led her toward the dance floor and nearly jerked her into his arms. "Are you mad?" he whispered furiously.

"I must be to want to have anything to do with you. My God, you're rude. Couldn't you at least have said something to him? He was only trying to help."

"How? By irrevocably linking my name to his? How could you show up here with him?"

"I had my reasons."

He had a response ready for that, but they were drawn deeper into the center of the dance floor and several people who'd heard him say Rennie couldn't come were already eyeing them with curiosity. They forced themselves to exchange greetings and Rennie briefly tried out her fabricated story about being caught up in a business meeting, while Nate used the time to regain control of his temper. It wasn't as difficult as he imagined since holding her had a more potent calming effect than even he'd anticipated.

"You got that dress from the apartment, didn't you?" he asked gruffly, as once again he edged them closer to the outer circle of the crowd.

"I snuck in early this morning after you'd already left."

She'd left no trace, he mused. Was it because he'd been preoccupied—or because she hadn't taken anything but the dress?

"Worried?" she asked sweetly.

"What's that supposed to mean?"

"You needn't pretend any longer, Nate. I found the compact by the couch. You know, the one with Madeline's name engraved inside?"

"Why, Rennie! This is delightful. Nate told us you wouldn't be able to come."

They both turned, startled to see Wendell and Maggie beside them. "Well, I managed to get out of my meeting after all," Rennie told them, forcing a bright smile. She focused on Maggie's gown, a creation of chocolate-brown lace over satin. "You look wonderful. Obviously you're feeling better?"

"It was just the flu," Wendell said before his wife could respond, easing her into Nate's arms and drawing Rennie into his own. "Let me steal this lovely creature from you for a few moments, Nate."

Before anyone had a chance to react, Wendell

whisked her away while Maggie recovered enough to warn him to remember his blood pressure. "If I listened to everything that old buzzard doctor of mine said, I'd be six feet under already," he grumbled.

Rennie glanced up at his flushed face and bit her lip. She might be grateful to have a moment's reprieve from having to talk to Nate, but obviously Maggie was right to worry about her husband. He didn't look well at all. "Why don't you take me to where the champagne is?" she said gently. "I don't know about you, but I could use something cool to drink."

"Of course, my dear. This way. You know, I haven't told you how glad I am about you and Nate. He's a fine man. We have our differences, as I'm sure he's told you, but way down deep we're just like family. Yes, indeed."

It took Nate a half hour to corner Rennie again, and the next time he drew her onto the dance floor, they were far more quiet and far more wary of each other's temperament. As the band played a slow bluesy number, he thought of all the things they needed to talk about, but he couldn't bring himself to mention any of them. He didn't want to risk ruining this peaceful moment, tentative though it was.

"I haven't yet told you how radiant you look," he murmured at last. "Is that what being away from me does for you?"

"You sent me away," she whispered, turning her head to avoid even the touch of his breath against her forehead.

"I wanted you off the case, not out of my life."

"That wasn't an option."

"Rennie—"

"Where's Madeline?" she asked brightly. She tossed her head back to look at him, challenge in her eyes. "Under the circumstances, I would think she'd be joining you here tonight."

Nate slid his hand up her back, under the silky fall of her hair. "Well, you're wrong. Madeline committed herself to a drug rehabilitation clinic this afternoon. I took her myself."

Nothing he could have said would have surprised her more. "I don't understand. I thought she wasn't anywhere near ready to admit she had a problem."

"I finally managed to convince her otherwise."

"Congratulations. I'm sure you gave her a worthy incentive."

"Nothing happened between us, Rennie."

She attempted a nonchalant shrug and failed. "At any rate, it's none of my business."

"Damn it—" He glanced around before exhaling heavily. "Please. Can we not argue for a moment? Will you just listen to me? *Yes*, she came over last night; and, yes, she made a pass.

But she was higher than those balloons they send up to check atmospheric conditions. She promptly passed out on my couch, and when she came to this morning, I gave her the lecture she's been needing for a long time. I won't say I expected her to listen to me, but she did—and she broke down. Afterward, as I said, I drove her to the clinic myself."

Ashamed, Rennie stared at his bow tie. "I'm sorry for acting shrewish. It was good of you to be there for her. Maybe when she gets out you can pick up the pieces and put your relationship back together again."

Nate just barely held his temper in check. "There isn't anything to put back together. I've told you before that whatever feelings I had for her changed a long time ago. What concerns me now is *us*. Rennie, is it that unforgivable for me to think of you as a woman first and an investigator second?"

"I only want to help you."

"What do you think I'm trying to do for *you*?" he demanded gruffly. He managed a crooked smile. "What do you suppose a psychiatrist would make of that?"

"Don't make a joke out of it."

"Sweetheart, I'm dying here. Comedy is the farthest thing from my mind." He stopped them at the mezzanine stairs, which also led out to the gardens. His look was entreating. "I know it's cold outside, but if I lend you my jacket, could we just go out for a minute or two and talk?''

He didn't wait for an answer, nor did she bother trying to refuse. They both knew there were too many people around to do any serious talking, so they hurried up the stairs, slipped around some of the gaily set green-and-white tables, then an exquisite urn filled with exotic flowers and peacock feathers to exit by a side door.

The wind had died down somewhat, but the air was brisk, the stars sharply in focus in the indigo sky. As he'd promised, Nate immediately slipped out of his jacket and wrapped her in it.

"You always seem to be doing this for me,'' she murmured, suddenly feeling a rush of shyness. "I don't know why you don't have a habitual case of the sniffles.''

He drew her into a corner where lattice and ivy protected them from some of the cold and anyone who might have similar ideas about stealing a few moments of privacy. "Hold me and I'll have all the warmth I need.''

She slipped her arms around his waist and rested her cheek against his chest. All right, she thought, feeling his strong arms come around her; maybe there was a time for everything after all, and maybe this was their time to stop fighting each other and just yield to the peace and the tenderness. He smelled so good in this crisp, cold air.

When she chuckled softly, he twisted his head to frown down at her. "What?"

"I just had a silly thought. I was thinking that you smelled good, crisp, you know? But all I can associate with crisp at the moment is lettuce. Not very romantic, huh?"

"Mmm." He tried not to laugh but it rumbled in his chest. "You definitely need some tutoring."

"I'll admit it's been a while since I've found myself in this kind of situation."

"Let me help." He lowered his cheek and rested it against hers. "Feel this? When I've been going to sleep lately, I've pretended we're like this, only lying down so we're touching everywhere. Even our toes seek out each other, but they mess around and do silly things because toes are kind of ticklish, know what I mean?"

"Nate, toes are about as romantic as lettuce."

"Oh, no," he murmured, inching his lips to the delicate shell of her ear. He traced its fragile shape before nipping it gently with his teeth. "They just have the misfortune to be way down there—the last to know whenever something is going on. But after a while when they warm up and catch on to how fingers are having all that fun, toes are about as sexy as—"

"Uh, wait...I think I get the picture." She tilted back her head to allow him better access to her throat.

"Then I'll get back to my story. There we are lying in bed wrapped around each other like wild rose vines."

"They have stickers."

"And *you* have a too literal mind." He inched his mouth back up toward her lips. "Close your eyes tighter and concentrate."

"Stickers are stickers."

He laughed again, charmed even as she exasperated him. "Well, think of a vine that doesn't have thorns."

"Morning glories, I suppose, jasmine...oh, and wild honeysuckle is nice and it smells good, too."

"Good. Then think of honeysuckle vines," he murmured tracing the shape of her lips with his once, and then again. "Sun kissed, fragrant honeysuckle with a drop of nectar on the inside of each blossom."

She stared up at his beautifully sculpted mouth and drew in an unsteady breath. "Would it be sweet?"

"Incredibly. Come here and I'll show you."

He offered his mouth and she explored him tentatively, even shyly with her tongue, half expecting him to force her into more. When it didn't happen, she deepened the kiss herself and felt him catch his breath. His heart began to pound heavily against her breasts. It was gentle, yet sensuous, and so unlike anything she'd ever experienced, she drew back to study his face in the darkness.

"What's wrong?" he whispered gruffly, struggling to ignore the ache that was beginning to throb deep inside him.

"I once wondered about us doing this, wondered what it would feel like."

"And?"

"You make me want so much more."

He exhaled shakily and sought her lips again. "Rennie..."

A high-pitched beeping sound pierced their quiet shell. Rennie muttered under her breath and fumbled with her purse.

"Damn—its my pager. I'm sorry, but I have to call in."

"We could do it from my place."

She didn't know what to say. She wanted to be with him, but a part of her still wondered if she could bear taking the risk of opening her heart again. "Let me call in first," she said, slipping off his jacket and handing it to him.

"If you don't mind, I'll stay out here a minute or two and—uh—enjoy the cool air." He needed the time alone to get his body back under control. But he brushed the backs of his fingers against her cheek. "Will you come right back?"

"Yes."

He watched her go in, then walked out to the end of the patio that overlooked the gardens. It

was the wrong time of year for flowers and foun-
tains, and the new moon made it too dark to see
more than the shadow of carefully tended shrub-
bery. But he didn't mind. He really wasn't interested in looking at the grounds anyway; he was
thinking about Rennie and what they'd just
shared.

That was why he didn't see the shadow that
separated itself from the others, but rather turned
around to look back into the ballroom. She hadn't
been gone more than a minute and already he
was restless to have her back.

Funny how he hadn't felt the cold until she
went in. He drew on his jacket and slid up the
sleeve to check his watch. Crackling leaves—beside him? No, behind him—caught his attention.
He turned, but not soon enough.

Something came over his head and he vaguely
noticed a flash of white—a sleeve—then thou-
sands of stars exploding before his eyes.

Chapter Eight

He couldn't breathe.

He was dying.

The thoughts came with blinding clarity and, with the fierce instincts of a man who had just tasted life at its sweetest, he fought them. He swung back at his assailant with one hand while trying to remove the excruciatingly tight cord around his neck with the other.

It didn't budge.

No one was behind him.

Help, get help, a panicked voice inside him screamed. He lurched toward the ballroom doors. Only yards away, they seemed like miles and each step cost him precious air. Still trying to tear the cord from his throat, he reached for the doorknob, missed, and fumbled again. Fire seared his lungs and his throat.

Inside, people strolled by oblivious of his agony.

A couple stopped; the woman's face distorted into a scream, just as he wrenched the door open. Yelling, screaming and music merged creating a din that echoed in his ears, and he fell, tangled in his own legs, betrayed by his confused senses.

He was only vaguely aware of people surrounding him, trying to help. They only made things worse. The pressure built. His chest and head were threatening to explode. Darkness began to close in...

"I got it!"

He heard the satisfaction in the voice more than he understood the words. But whatever "I got it" meant, he knew *he* had it, too. Air. Sweet, wonderful air rushing into his lungs and pulling him back from the darkness. He drew on it greedily and broke into a hacking cough.

"Easy, mister. There's plenty more where that came from."

Someone began to roll him onto his back. He caught sight of a white sleeve and immediately struck out, ready to defend himself.

"Hey! I said it's okay. I'm the one who just cut you loose."

Nate had to blink several times before the young waiter holding the small opened pocket-knife came into focus...and then the countless other faces staring down at him with various expressions of shock and concern. Someone else shoved their way into the circle and dropped down beside the young man. Great legs, he thought as he viewed what was generously exposed by the parting bronze gown. If he hadn't felt as lousy as he did, he might have laughed, for it came to him in that untimely moment that there was always going to be one way by which he would be able to recognize her.

"Nate—oh, God, Nate!"

She blocked out everything and everyone as she leaned over him to touch his cheek, his throat, his hair. She was rambling and her voice broke every few words, but he didn't care. It was her eyes he was focusing on; and what he saw there almost made this nightmare worth it.

"Rennie," he rasped, covering the trembling hand at his cheek with his own.

"Yes, darling. It's me." She turned to the young man beside her. "Get the police—and call for an ambulance. Please! Will everyone move back and give us some room? Oh, Nate," she whispered, turning back to press her cheek to his. "I should never have left you."

"S'okay," he repeated the waiter's words, closing his eyes to absorb the feel of her. Unlike her, he didn't give a damn if they had an audience or not. He'd seen the truth of her feelings for him in her eyes and nothing and no one else mattered. "Just don't leave me now."

"I'm not going anywhere. Can you sit up?"

He would sprout wings and fly; she had only to ask. But she slipped her arm around his back instead and he struggled to an upright position, hampered only slightly by another coughing spasm.

"Let us through, please! I must get through!" With Maggie in tow, Wendell finally broke through the line of onlookers. When he caught sight of Nate, he swayed and grasped his wife's arm with both hands.

"Maggie, you'd better get him home. I think he looks worse than I do," Nate said, eyeing his partner's shattered expression.

"Listen to him." Wendell's laugh was forced. "Always the kidder. You had us worried." He reached into his jacket and drew out a handkerchief to wipe away the moisture collecting on his forehead and upper lip.

"Had myself worried, too."

"What in heaven's name happened?"

"That's exactly what I was about to ask," Jim Killian said, making his own way into the circle. "I was out front checking in with the boys on duty," he explained upon catching Nate's raised eyebrow. He glanced around at the crowd and grimaced. "We'd better move to someplace where we can talk."

"I'm the manager," someone called. "Use my office."

With Killian's assistance, Rennie helped Nate to his feet and they followed the club's manager out of the ballroom and across the lobby to the small but private room. She insisted Nate lie down on the leather couch. He did, but he also grabbed her hand and drew her down beside him. Wendell tried to enter with Maggie, however his attempt was politely, but firmly, thwarted by Killian.

"We've phoned for an ambulance and paramedics," the manager told them. "Is there anything I can get anyone before I leave you?"

"Water," Nate said hoarsely, pulling open his bow tie.

"Fresh on the credenza." The manager indicated the tray bearing the decanter and clean glasses to Rennie before closing the door behind himself.

She poured Nate a glass while Killian removed his coat and laid it over a chair. "Here," she said, returning a moment later. She held the glass to his lips and a hand under his chin, clucking in disapproval when he drank greedily. "Take your time. You don't want to have another coughing seizure."

"On the other hand look at all the attention I'm getting."

"Any more cracks like that and you might end up wearing this water instead of drinking it."

Nate gave Killian an unworried look. "Reaction."

"It happens."

Ignoring them, Rennie loosened the top two buttons on his shirt, wincing as she studied the raw wound around his neck. "What did he use on you, wire?"

"A nylon electrical tie," Killian said, unfolding his handkerchief and gingerly holding up the evidence he'd picked up from the carpet. "I imagine if there were any prints on this, they've been smudged by you and that waiter. Effective little gizmo. Operates much the same as a garbage tie; once it's cinched, it's unremovable unless you cut it off. Lucky for you that kid had a pocketknife on him."

"Hideous." Rennie shivered, repulsed. "Did you have a chance to see who it was?" she asked Nate.

"It was too dark…and he was too quick." He paused to swallow. "All I saw was a sleeve. It was just like the boy's."

"You mean the waiter's?" Rennie shot a look at Killian. "Are you saying he was dressed as a waiter?"

"I'm not sure, but the buttons—the gold buttons and the white sleeve were the same."

Killian went to the door and drew in one of his people. "Don't let any of the waiters leave, and get someone to check the area for more of these ties or anything else the perpetrator might have left behind.''

Nate turned his attention back to Rennie who was worrying her lower lip with her teeth. He took both her hands in his and placed a kiss on the backs of each. "Hey, it's over. I'm all right."

"But don't you understand? He was out there with us."

"Maybe. I don't know. I think he only got there after you went inside."

Rennie looked away, her eyes shadowed by a haunting thought. "The rules have changed. He doesn't just want you out of Chicago, he wants you dead."

"I think she's right," Killian said, closing the door behind the departing policeman. "In fact I think the blackmailer's courier has become a lone wolf with a mission of his own."

"How do you figure that?" Nate asked.

"If the blackmailer had wanted you dead, he wouldn't have wasted time trying to intimidate you into leaving town. Any ideas who this other guy might be?"

"I'm still trying to figure out who'd want to chase me out of town; how am I supposed to know who's trying to *kill* me?"

"What about a man named Tilman?" Rennie saw the quick narrowing of his eyes. "Oh, God, you *do* know him."

"The question is, how do *you*?"

"I only heard his name for the first time this afternoon."

"From a mutual acquaintance, I'd wager," Nate drawled.

"Yes. I was told that he's been heard bragging about having a job, a contract to do something he would have done for free."

He sank back against the cushions and exhaled a long breath. "I guess it's possible." He glanced at Killian who stepped closer. "His full name is Len Tilman. I was instrumental in sending him to prison a few years ago when I got his ex-girlfriend to testify against him on behalf of my client in an extortion case. I wasn't at Tilman's trial, but I heard he went crazy and made some threats. You know that's not uncommon."

Killian nodded and drew out his notebook. "We'll put the word out. Maybe someone will spot—" There was a knock at the door and he opened it slightly. "Paramedics."

Nate submitted himself to an examination and was soon informed that he had indeed been lucky. There didn't appear to be any severe injury to his throat, however he was still advised to go to the hospital and that it wouldn't hurt to spend the night under observation.

"We're going home," he told the paramedic, though his eyes were on Rennie. "I'll get all the care I need there."

As he got up, she helped him back into his

jacket. "Is it all right if we leave now, Detective Killian?" she asked.

"I have a feeling if I said no, you'd ignore me anyway so go ahead. I'll arrange for you to have an escort, and we'll put someone outside the building for the night."

Minutes later they were pulling away from the country club in the car Nate had rented since his was going to take several days to service. Rennie insisted on driving and a patrol car followed at a discreet distance.

Nate was content to lie back against the headrest and watch her. The light from passing street lamps fleetingly illuminated her face, and though she continued to look pale, he thought she'd never seemed lovelier to him.

"What did DePalma say when you told him you were leaving with me?"

"He sent you his best wishes and reminded me that he was only a phone call away."

"Cute. I suppose I should be grateful to him for bringing you back to me," he muttered after a moment.

"At the least. Nate, if it wasn't for Mario DePalma, I would still be pounding the pavement looking for a lead on that photographer."

"I said I was grateful, didn't I?"

She saw the way his frown turned into a full-fledged scowl and smiled crookedly. "I haven't had a chance to ask you how your meeting with the Morgan Towers attorneys went.''

"We agreed to continue discussing the possibility of an out-of-court agreement.''

"Attorneys.'' Rennie shook her head at what she considered was nothing more than a lot of beating around the bush. "I think DePalma and Jerome should settle their disagreement between themselves.''

"One of them would probably end up sleeping with the fishes, my dear.''

"You people just like to think no one can settle problems without you. Speaking of attorneys, though, I couldn't help noticing that Wendell didn't look at all well tonight. I thought it was Maggie who was supposed to be ill?''

"I'm concerned, too. He's said his doctor has been on him to lose some weight and to get his blood pressure lowered, but he doesn't seem to be working on it. It didn't help things when Killian didn't let him in the manager's office, did it?''

"As your partner, I'm sure he felt he was within his rights to be with you.''

"Only because he was worried about losing the firm's biggest moneymaker.'' He reached over and toyed with a lock of her hair. "But that's hardly what I want to talk about.''

"You really shouldn't be talking at all. How's the throat? It sounds terribly raw and painful.''

"It only hurts when you interrupt me and try to change the subject."

Rennie pulled up to the electronic lock at the apartment building's parking garage entrance and slipped in the identification card Nate handed her. A moment later there was a buzz and the iron gates that provided night security slid open. She had an idea what subject Nate was accusing her of avoiding, but he couldn't be more wrong. As she pulled into a parking spot and shut off the engine, she turned to tell him so.

"I'm not trying to change the subject. I *want* to talk, to be here with you. Tonight when I saw you lying there, when I realized what could have happened, it made me realize what a fool I was being—and what a coward."

Nate leaned forward and pressed a finger to her lips. "Wait a minute. You are a lot of things, Rennie Paris, but a coward isn't one of them." As she began to disagree, he leaned forward and gave her a quick kiss. "Let's go upstairs and we can debate the issue to your heart's content."

They walked arm in arm to the elevator. On the ride up Rennie rested her head against his shoulder feeling a strange but exciting sense of homecoming.

She was through with fighting her heart. Tonight was a new beginning. Whatever happened, she would face it honestly.

"You're so quiet," Nate murmured, as the car

reached his floor. "Are the nerves setting in already?"

"No. Well, a little," she admitted, thinking of the promise she'd just made to herself. Her brief laugh held embarrassment. "I've told you before, I'm so out of practice with dating and everything—I feel like a teenager."

He slipped his arm around her waist and led her down the hallway to his door. "This isn't a date, sweetheart. This is our beginning; but I don't want you to feel anything is going to happen that you aren't ready for."

He unlocked the door and they went inside. The lamp on his desk lit their way into the living room and cast a soft inviting glow. As she laid her purse and coat on a nearby chair, Rennie smiled to herself when she realized how good it felt to be back.

"What?" Nate demanded, removing his own jacket.

"I'm getting spoiled. My apartment is nothing like this. The only thing you lack here is a fireplace."

"I'll have someone come out tomorrow and we'll see what we can do." He came to her and slowly drew her into his arms. As he noticed her bemused expression a smile played around his lips, but his eyes were dark with deeper emotions. "Don't you know by now that I would do just about anything to make you happy?"

"Why?" she asked, needing the reassurance despite her enchantment.

"For starters how about because you turn me on?"

"My looks aren't anything special."

"Crazy woman." He turned her back into the entryway and held her in front of the wall mirror. They created a dramatic picture in the semidarkness. "Look," he whispered, gently massaging her shoulders. "I've been waiting for you to put on this dress since the moment I saw you hanging it up that day in your room. Even then I knew it was perfect for you." He trailed his fingers down her bare arms and then back up again. "You look like a flame, captivating, warm and inviting."

Rennie eased her body back against his and reached up to touch his cheek. "And you have a romantic soul. I've never met anyone who made me want to believe in fairy tales before."

"This isn't a fairy tale." He turned her around to face him and framed her face with his hands. "This is as real as we want it to be; and I want... Rennie, dear God, I just want."

His kiss was as light as his touch, entreating, coaxing. He skimmed his lips over hers, tasting her briefly, before moving on to explore her uptilted face. She watched him as long as she could. It made him smile and he purposely kissed both of her eyes closed.

"But I love to watch you," she whispered in

protest. "Your face changes, hardens, and here there's a line like a lightning bolt." She traced her fingers over his jaw, his cheekbones and finally the spot between his eyebrows.

"It's your fault."

"How so?"

"Your reaction when I touch you is always so sweet, so honest it arouses me before I realize what's happening. I know if I don't hold back, I'll be tempted to just take what I want."

Her body trembled in reaction and she felt his fingers tighten as he felt it. "Kiss me like that. I don't want you to hold back anymore. Take what you want."

He whispered her name before claiming her mouth with his, and a moan broke from him as she met his tongue with hers to match his hungry stroking with her own. He explored her, teased and dared her. Then he angled his head in the opposite direction and began all over again.

He drew the very breath out of her and, finally, she was forced to pull away. Her eyes closed, she gasped for air. "When are you supposed to breathe?"

"I'm not sure I've figured that out myself," he replied, almost as breathless. "This—total preoccupation is a new experience for me, too." When she opened her eyes to give him a skeptical look, he swore. "What is it going to take to make you believe no woman has ever affected me the way you have? Feel me," he rasped, bringing her body totally against his. "All we've done is kiss and I'm already close to the edge."

There was no mistaking the tautness of his body and Rennie moaned softly as he lowered his hands to her hips and pressed himself even deeper into her warmth. Then she brushed her lips against the side of his neck. "You're—um, going to get closer now."

"Little witch." He laughed huskily before dragging in a deep breath. "Do you realize we're still standing by the front door?"

She understood what he was doing; he was trying to bank his own desire in order to give her time to decide what she wanted. But she already knew what that was; she wanted *him*. She wanted to spend the rest of her life like this, in his arms.

Her decision made, she lifted her head and gently nipped his chin. "Whose fault is that?" she teased.

He narrowed his eyes, searching hers for any sign that he might be misinterpreting what he saw, then took her hand and drew her into the living room. "Definitely mine, otherwise why on earth would we be standing when I want to be here with you," he murmured, lowering her to the couch. As she slipped her arms around his neck to make sure he followed her, he smiled.

"I love the feel of you against me," she whispered, stretching. "You're so warm."

"Heavy?"

"Yes, but—oh, Nate, it's such a delicious feeling."

He uttered an oath and sought her mouth again. She made him ache, but he knew they would both be long past aching before he even began to sate himself with the taste and feel of her. It would take years, he thought, a lifetime. Burying one hand in her hair, he slid the other beneath her and lifted her into the tender but seductive rotation of his hips.

Rennie felt pressure flood her senses and arched closer. She wanted more, she wanted everything he would give her and unhesitatingly reached between them to unbutton his shirt. His chest was matted with dark, crisp hair that drew her fingers. She splayed them through it and felt the powerful beating of his heart, his heat and the tautness of his muscles. She wanted to draw him against her, but he resisted.

"This will make it better," he said, reaching for the zipper at her nape.

He was watching her closely and she knew he could tell what she was thinking. She was wearing little beneath her dress and she was about to expose more to him than she had to any man except her doctor in years. But this was Nate and hadn't he already made her feel beautiful? She trusted him. Most important, however, was the realization that she was ready to accept her love for him.

She smiled into his eyes.

The zipper descended. Cool air touched her back, and Nate placed a reassuring kiss on her forehead before drawing her gown down over her shoulders to her waist. Then he was lowering himself to her and she felt the strength of him and the warmth, merging with hers.

"Rennie," he whispered in her ear. "Sweet heaven, I could die now and be content."

"Why didn't you tell me sooner that you'd be so easy to please?"

He burst into laughter and hugged her fiercely. "Stop it, will you? I'm being serious."

"So am I."

He raised himself on one elbow and stared incredulously at her. "You are, aren't you?"

"I'm the woman whose husband once compared her to a palm tree minus the fruit."

"The fruit?"

"Coconuts."

"Hmm." Nate shifted slightly and took a deep breath. "Darling, the man obviously didn't understand that quality transcends quantity."

Rennie secured her arms more tightly around him. "Obviously."

Nate brushed his lips against hers. "Believe it."

She wanted to. She wanted to believe in everything again: Christmas, romance, but most of all love. As he slid down her body and closed his mouth over her breast, she felt the ardent stroking of his tongue and knew, with him, even a little of anything would be a banquet to her.

She tangled her fingers in his hair and drew him closer. He deepened the ministrations of his mouth, and shifted his hand so that he could tease the taut peak of her other breast. Sweetness pierced through her and she caught her breath, then exhaled on a trembling sigh.

Such gentleness, she thought, feeling the care beneath his caresses. How could a man who had just suffered at the hands of violence find such gentleness inside himself? He made her feel so special, so cherished. She wanted him to know that same feeling.

She drew him back to her mouth and gave him everything that was in her heart and soul. For an instant, a heartbeat, he stiffened, then he traced his fingers up her rib cage, over the gentle swell of her breast to touch her face wonderingly.

"Rennie?"

"Make love with me," she whispered against his lips. "I want to belong to you, be a part of you."

"You already are. Here," he replied, taking her hand and pressing it to his heart. "The rest— We can wait, sweetheart. We don't have to rush things."

"But I thought you wanted me?"

He tightened his hold on her. His expression hardened and became almost fierce. "I ache with wanting you. But I want you to be sure. Once I take you, I won't let you go. This isn't going to be just sex, Rennie. Are you sure?" he asked with the slightest lift of his eyebrow.

"Yes, I'm sure," she whispered, tightening her arms. "Never let me go. Especially not tonight."

He looked down to watch as she brought their bodies together, saw her taut nipples still moist from his kisses and closed his eyes at the beauty of it, the delicious feel of it. "Never," he vowed touching his mouth to hers.

As the kiss deepened to passionate, the phone rang, dragging moans from both of them. Nate buried his face in Rennie's hair and she stared up at the ceiling in disbelief.

"I vote we ignore it and maybe whoever that is will get the idea and hang up," he muttered. But after another moment someone began knocking at the front door as well. Nate sat up, his opinion of the situation capsulized by one hoarse oath. "What is this, a convention?"

"Maybe we'd better see what's going on," Rennie said, already beginning to rearrange her clothes. "Why don't you get the phone and I'll answer the door."

Nate resisted a moment longer, his gaze possessive as he watched her draw her gown up over her breasts. "All I can say is the damned building better be on fire," he growled, heading for the phone.

Rennie's sense of humor was already returning, and she was chuckling softly by the time she finished zipping up her gown and hurrying to the door. But when she peered through the security hole and saw who was standing there, a frown replaced the smile on her face. She quickly unlocked the door.

"Albert...Faith...what in the world is going on?"

Chapter Nine

Nudged by his wife, Albert cleared his throat and nodded to Rennie. "I need to talk to Nate."

"We know it's a terrible hour to be calling on you," Faith injected. "Particularly considering what happened at the ball. Maggie and Wendell told us," she explained when Rennie gave her a surprised look. "But Albert's right, we do need to speak with Nate."

"Of course, come in." She stepped back, though she was still confused. She self-consciously tucked her hair behind her ears. "What I don't understand is what are you still doing here in Chicago? Weren't you supposed to leave tonight and be gone until Sunday?"

"Yes, but— Well, something's come up and we decided it was more important to be here.

Hello, Nate,'' Faith said as he joined them. "We were sorry to hear about what happened. How are you feeling?"

He was tempted to tell her, however he knew she was hardly inquiring after *that* part of his physical condition. He ran a hand along the front of the shirt he'd hastily rebuttoned and shot Rennie a conspiratorial look. "Fine. That was security on the phone just now. They thought it best to announce your arrival, especially since you said that seeing me was a matter of life and death—namely mine."

"What?" Rennie tore her gaze from him to stare at the couple. "Please sit down. Tell us what's wrong."

"I'll stand, if you don't mind," Albert said, as his wife took a seat on one of the chairs. Neither of them removed their coats. "I wouldn't turn down a drink, though. Scotch or brandy, whatever you have."

Because Wendell's son rarely indulged in any form of alcohol, Nate caught himself stiffening. But he recovered quickly enough to play amenable host and asked the ladies if they would have anything, before going to get the brandy.

When he returned Faith was complimenting Rennie on her dress, but he could tell that her effusive rambling was mostly from nerves. He handed Albert the snifter and sat down on the arm of Rennie's chair. If there was going to be trouble—of any kind—he wanted to be near her. She already looked as tense as he felt.

"All right, you have our undivided attention," he said, gruffly. "Have you come to confess or warn?"

Albert met his sharp gaze without blanching, but his skin seemed to take on a gray tinge. Never a handsome man, he looked as though he'd aged a decade overnight. A pronounced hint of gray made his nondescript brown hair even duller, and there were sharp lines around his gray eyes and thin mouth. Even his raincoat hung on his slumped shoulders as though it, too, was world-weary.

"Nate—I know we've never been what you'd call friends, but I want you to know that despite everything, I've always respected you. I would never, nor have I ever, done anything to endanger you personally, or threaten you professionally."

"But you know someone who has."

"Yes." With a pained look at his wife, Albert turned away and after taking a deep swallow of his drink, he ran his hand through his hair. Its mussed state suggested it had seen that action more than once tonight. "God, Faith...I don't think I can do it."

"You have to." She rose and went to him, grasping his hand in a gesture of support. "You've come this far, and you *know* it's the right thing to do."

"I feel like I'm betraying him."

"*He* betrayed *you*, all of us, by putting us in this position." She turned to Nate. "He's trying to tell you that Wendell is the person blackmailing you."

Without consciously thinking of it, Rennie placed a soothing hand on Nate's thigh. He placed his own hand over hers and gave it a reassuring squeeze.

"Go on," he said flatly.

"Please understand, he's ill. The doctors are saying he's going to need surgery, and even then... It's his heart. To make matters worse, he's convinced he wouldn't survive the operation. It's been plaguing his mind for weeks now."

"I don't get it; what does that have to do with blackmailing me?"

Faith turned back to her husband and gave him a pleading look. He placed the barely touched drink on a side table and swung around to face Nate.

"Don't you understand? He's decided to get his house in order. He wants to leave things as near to his idea of perfect as he can get them. He'd succeeded with everything except my future."

Nate stared at him for a moment before bursting into laughter. No, he thought, it was simply too ridiculous. "Are you going to try to tell me it was this partnership thing all along? He's blackmailing me because I wouldn't agree to make you a partner in the firm? Good grief, with what your inheritance would be, you could open your *own* damned firm.''

"It was *this* firm he wanted; to him it's like a legacy to pass down through the generations of Dillards to come.''

"What generations?'' Nate asked sarcastically.

"Nate.''

He glanced over to Rennie, saw the entreaty in her eyes and grimaced. She was right, of course; it served no purpose to insult the messenger, particularly under these circumstances. But the whole thing was ludicrous and he told Albert so.

"Why didn't he simply come to me and tell me that he was ill and what it was he wanted?''

"Would you have given me the partnership?''

"Under certain conditions, possibly. You're no trial lawyer, but you have an eye for detail and analysis. If you had managed to stop your father from trying to turn you into a Perry Mason for five minutes, we might have developed you into a first-class corporate attorney.''

"I'm sure you mean that as a compliment,'' Albert replied with quiet dignity, "but I'm no more interested in that than I am in what my father aspired for me. In fact you'll have my resignation on your desk tomorrow morning.'' He looked toward Faith. "I think it's about time that

I started living my own life, and it doesn't include continuing with a job I despise."

"You're going to give your old man a stroke."

"As a matter of fact, my father is in the hospital right now. He suffered a mild seizure tonight after returning home from the ball."

Nate winced. "Hell. I'm sorry."

Albert shrugged off the apology. "You'd better know the whole story. You see, I've been aware he was up to something for several days now. He was upset, short-tempered and paranoid.

"Earlier this evening there'd been a phone call. I answered and the caller obviously thought I was my father. What little he said confirmed my suspicions that Dad was involved with something way over his head. I called him into the study and insisted he tell me what was wrong. He denied anything was, of course, and shortly afterward left with my mother."

"Albert was terribly upset," Faith assured Nate and Rennie. "He knew he had to get to the bottom of this, so we decided to delay our trip and wait for Wendell and Maggie to return home."

"The fight was out of him," Albert continued numbly. "I didn't even have to ask, he simply broke down and told us the whole story. But what he didn't anticipate was losing control over that—"

A sharp knock interrupted him. Nate and Rennie exchanged quizzical glances and, placing a restraining hand on her shoulder, he went to answer it.

"Killian, don't you ever go to bed?" he muttered, even before he had the door completely opened.

"I might be able to if you stopped stirring up all this activity." The detective sauntered into the living room looking fatigued but determined. He nodded to Rennie before giving the Dillards his full attention. "I was almost home when I got an interesting message on the radio. It seems the security guard downstairs alerted our man outside about the distraught couple who were headed up to this apartment."

"This is Detective Killian who's been working the case," Rennie told them, then introduced them to the detective. "Albert is Wendell's son, and he's just told us that Wendell is the person who originated the idea of the blackmail."

"But my father never intended to harm Nate," Albert insisted. "That must be understood. In fact, if Nate had simply ignored the situation and—and that person Dad hired hadn't gone crazy on him, my father would probably have realized how foolish he was being and dropped the whole thing. He understands now."

"That makes me feel a lot better," the detective drawled. "How about you, Montgomery?"

"Go on with your story, Albert," Rennie said,

shooting Killian an impatient look. "Your father discovered he was ill and he wanted to settle certain things, so he hired Len Tilman to find a photographer that could doctor some photographs."

"My God...you know about Tilman?"

"We're only beginning to piece things together. What we don't know is how your father found Tilman in the first place."

"He didn't. Tilman found *him*. It was at a bar where my father was negotiating a deal with an—er, agreeable darkroom technician. Tilman overheard and offered to handle the whole thing for him. At the time, my father didn't know Nate had once helped put Tilman behind bars; he didn't find that out until the night you were almost run over in the garage. After that he tried to call it off. All of it. But Tilman just laughed at him and said no way. He even started extorting money from my father. He said if he didn't pay him an additional twenty thousand dollars, he'd see that the police heard about the scheme himself."

"What a mess," sighed Rennie.

Killian pulled his earlobe. "Yeah, well, when you step off the sidewalk into the sewer you gotta expect—"

"How about offering some advice instead of philosophy." Nate shot him a hard look then gave a more compassionate one to Faith who was as pale as chalk, yet stood resolutely beside her husband. His admiration for her had grown considerably in the past few minutes. In her own way, she was as strong as Rennie; he hoped Albert realized how lucky he was. He was only beginning to appreciate his own good fortune.

"Advice." Killian dipped his hands into the pockets of his wrinkled coat and toyed with some loose change. "My advice is that we'd better find Tilman before he succeeds in playing out this vendetta of his. We've got an all-points bulletin out on him, but he's a slippery fish. Any suggestions as to where to look, Mr. Dillard?"

"My father told me about the bar where Tilman hangs out. It's on the South Side. It's where they met and where he had to deliver the initial payment. I don't remember the name—wait. It has to do with spices, I think...yes, Peppers."

"I know it," Rennie said. "It's almost under the tracks. Not exactly Wendell's type of neighborhood."

Albert inclined his head. "He hated going there. He was afraid of getting mugged. As it is, he lost a couple of hubcaps on the car, and his radio."

"He should consider himself lucky," she replied gently. "Do you know if Tilman might be there now?"

"He has to be. My father was supposed to meet him there after the ball tonight to pay off the twenty thousand. If he doesn't show, Tilman said he'll come looking for him."

Rennie got up from the chair and began to pace around the room. A germ of an idea was spawning in her mind and, as she ran a finger along her lower lip, she formulated it into a plan. It would be risky, she acknowledged, but it could also mean that this entire episode would be over for Nate. That alone merited its consideration.

"I suggest we don't disappoint Mr. Tilman," she said, swinging back to the group. She wasn't at all surprised to see she had both Nate's and Killian's attention, but she focused on the detective because she knew she would need him as an ally. "I propose we set him up."

Albert shook his head. "How can you? My father was taken to the hospital less than an hour ago."

"You can go in his place."

"What?"

"You can keep the appointment with Tilman. Tell him the truth—that your father is ill and that you're willing to follow through with the commitment, but you can't get the money until tomorrow."

"Now just a minute," Albert began. "There's no way I'm going in there with news like that, especially not alone."

"You won't be alone. I'll be there to give you backup."

"Over my dead body," Nate announced.

"Wait a minute. She may be on to something

here,'' Killian said, still watching Rennie. ''What do you have in mind? You don't look like you belong in that neighborhood any more than Dillard does.''

''Give me ten minutes to change and I'll bet I can convince you otherwise. When I mosey into that bar, I'll just look like another hardworking girl taking a break. My guess is that after Albert delivers his bad news, Tilman will be so depressed, he'll want something—or rather, someone—to take his mind off his troubles. That's where I come in. I'll invite him to my place, and when we walk out of the bar together, you and your people can be there waiting to take him.''

''Forget it,'' Nate told her. ''It's too risky.''

''It's riskier to try to take him while he's still in the bar. We don't want any outsiders getting hurt,'' Killian told him.

''Then use one of your own people!''

''That would take time that we don't have.'' Killian turned back to Rennie. ''The only thing is that we'd have a better chance of making this extortion charge stick if we have evidence that Dillard actually handed over some money.''

''Fine. Scrounge up what we can between us. It'll make Albert look like he's trying to deal in good faith. You take care of that and I'll be right back.''

As she began to head for her room, Nate

grabbed her arm. "Rennie, for God's sake, you can't do this."

"He's right," Faith said. "I'm not sure I like the idea of Albert going into a place like that with a known criminal, but it would be even worse for you."

"Faith, I'm a private investigator. Believe me, I've played out worse scenarios; if we all do our jobs, and stay calm, everything will work out fine." She saw the other woman's shock and gave her an apologetic smile. "I'm sorry we had to deceive you, but when Nate hired me, we had to assume that everyone was a suspect."

"I—yes, I suppose I can understand that. But... does that mean you two were only pretending to be— Oh, dear. I'm sorry, it's really none of my business."

Rennie looked up at Nate and thought of what they would be doing right now if Faith and Albert hadn't knocked at the door. She thought of how far they'd come over the past two years, and how far they still had to go. But they weren't going to get anywhere if he couldn't trust her decisions and allow her to do what she felt was right.

"That's all right," she said quietly. "And no, actually, we weren't pretending at all. But Nate's also my best friend, and he understands that sometimes I have to do things in my own way.

Now if you'll all excuse me, I have to hurry and change.''

She half expected Nate to follow her into the guest bedroom, but he didn't. Less than fifteen minutes later she returned to find he'd poured himself a drink and was just finishing it off.

His eyes smoldered as they swept over her. Gone were the carefully combed curls, the subdued makeup and the expensive gown. In its place was a creature no less intriguing but far less subtle. Her hair was a wild mane falling around the short rabbit-fur jacket, her makeup was accented by dark liner, stark blusher and lots of lip gloss. It was the same outfit she'd worn the night she came home and pulled a gun on him. Nate found himself wondering if she was wearing as little beneath it as she had been that night, and then vowed that he would break Tilman's hands himself if he so much as touched her.

"All set," Killian said, hanging up the phone. "They'll have an envelope with some cash in it waiting for us when we get down there." He gave Rennie an appreciative nod. "You'll do. So, are we ready to go?"

"I'm going, too," Faith said, still holding Albert's arm.

"Lady—"

"So am I, Killian," added Nate.

The detective rubbed his whiskered jaw and shot a look of appeal at Rennie. "Listen, this isn't a taxi service I'm operating here, and the last thing I need is you two interfering with police business."

Nate held his ground. "We're going."

Killian threw up his hands and headed for the door. Faith took Albert's arm and went after him. As Rennie began to follow, Nate snatched his jacket, caught up with her in the entryway, and, as the others went down the hall, drew her back against a wall.

"You have to be the most stubborn woman I've ever met," he ground out, temper simmering only skin-deep.

"Please don't fight me on this, Nate."

"Fight you? I'd like to…I want to do lots of things with you, Rennie Paris, but fighting has never been one of them." He lifted a hand to stroke her cheek. "Why, sweetheart? Why are you so committed to doing this?"

She looked at the hair exposed in the open V of his shirt collar, the brass coatrack over his shoulder, anything but his eyes. "You know why."

He felt his heart stop. "Say it."

"Oh, Nate. I—"

"Hey!" Killian called from the elevators. "Let's move it."

"He's right. We have to go." Rennie quickly pressed a kiss on Nate's cheek and squeezed by him. "Coming!"

The bar was located in a run-down part of the city where shops were closed at night and secured by iron gates drawn across plate-glass windows. At this hour, people rarely walked alone, and if they did, it was with a speed and purpose to get off the streets as soon as possible.

Killian met two other patrol cars a half block down from the bar and pulled in behind them. As he got out to talk to the uniformed officers, Rennie and Nate stepped out into the crisp night air. Their breaths emerged as fleeting clouds of vapor that met and vanished under the harsh streetlights.

"You should have taken a heavier coat," she told him, thrusting her hands into her fur jacket. "If the weather keeps up like this, I think snow's going to come early this year."

Nerves. He heard them in her voice and wondered if they were for Tilman or himself. He took hold of the lapels of her jacket and decided to find out.

"Shut up and kiss me," he muttered, dragging her against him.

She felt everything as he half lifted her off her feet, his anger and his fear; but she was helpless to do anything about either, just as she couldn't resist burying her fingers deep into his hair and responding to the passionate kiss with equal honesty. She forgot the cold, the people nearby, the possible danger ahead. For a moment they were alone in the world and everything was utterly beautiful. But all too soon there was a discreet cough behind them.

"Sorry, guys, but it's showtime."

It took Rennie a moment to regain her balance. Nate continued to hold her by her coat lapels and she had to reach up and gently extricate his fingers one by one. All the while their gazes clung.

Finally she stepped away from him and looked past his shoulder to where Killian stood waiting. "Give me a few minutes before you send Albert in."

"Sure. Listen…I assume you're set for an emergency?"

She had to force herself to ignore Nate's sudden stiffening and patted her small shoulder bag. Then she turned on her heel and walked to the bar without a backward glance.

It took forever and gave her too much time to think and feel. She sensed Nate's eyes boring into her back and knew it was hurting him that she didn't turn around one last time. But she couldn't; seeing the fear, the torment in his eyes would be too much.

Fats Domino and clicking pool balls greeted her as she stepped inside the amber-lit bar. She resisted the urge to wrinkle her nose at the smell of stale smoke, but couldn't help narrowing her eyes against it as she scanned the room. A few people turned to see who'd walked in but, except for one brief whistle, they turned back to their conversations and to watching the wrestling match on TV.

Several people sat around the bar. Only one caught her attention and she went to the far side to take a seat two chairs away from him.

"Cold enough for you, honey?" the bartender asked, sliding a napkin in front of her.

"Yeah. Let me have a vodka on the rocks."

"Haven't seen you in here before."

"Who needs antifreeze in decent weather?" She gave the bartender an intimate smile and held it long enough to share it with the man she recognized as Len Tilman.

What a creep, she thought, taking in his slicked-back hair and sallow complexion, and how edgy. He shot her a resentful look before he turned his attention back to the front door. She understood; it was just past midnight, which meant he must have already been waiting here for the better part of an hour. If Albert walked in, he was going to get the full brunt of his annoyance.

As the bartender placed her drink before her and took the bill she'd laid out, she risked giving Tilman another friendly glance. "Care to buy a lady a drink?"

"You already got one."

"Maybe I'll want another. Anyway, I'm in no hurry."

"Well, I am."

Rennie drew her lips into a pout. "You don't look it to me."

"I'm waiting for somebody."

She tossed her head and took a sip of her drink. Great, she thought, just what she needed, a hard-nose. Swallowing her distaste along with the abhorrent liquor, she eased her jacket down her arms. The motion tugged her sweater off one shoulder and gave him a better view of what he was turning down.

"It doesn't look like she's going to show. Some women don't appreciate a good man when they find him."

At first she thought he was going to ignore her, but then he eyed her from beneath black brows. The look made her skin crawl.

"This is business, and maybe I have waited long enough. You have a place around here?"

"Close enough. Buy me one more drink and I might show you my teddy-bear collection."

Tilman smiled and began to motion for the bartender when his attention was drawn to the door behind her. She knew without looking that Albert had just walked in.

"What's the frown for?" Pretending to think his displeasure was with her, she glanced down at herself.

"Just be patient for a minute, green eyes. I

have a feeling my business appointment might be here after all.''

Albert made his way to the bar and sat down on the empty stool between them. She met his hesitant glance with a seductive smile and inwardly worried over the beads of sweat already forming on his brow.

''Are—are you Tilman?'' he asked as the bartender placed a napkin before him.

''Maybe. Order a drink.''

''I don't think I'd care for anything, thank you.''

''Hey, bud,'' the bartender said, clearly offended. ''You take up space, you order a drink.''

''Give him a brandy,'' Rennie purred. She stroked a finger down his coat sleeve. ''He looks like a brandy drinker to me.''

''Oh, y-yes. That would be fine. Thank you, ma'am. Miss.''

''The name's Rennie.''

''It's a pleasure to—''

''Hey!'' Tilman slapped his hand down on the bar and glared at Albert. ''Who *are* you, mister?''

''Albert...Albert Dillard. You have—you know my father. I know he was the one you were expecting, but he suffered a heart attack tonight and he's in the hospital. He asked me to come here in his place to reassure you that—that whatever deal you made with him will be honored.''

"Good. Then you brought the money?"

"No." Albert swallowed as Tilman's eyes narrowed to dangerous slits. "Please. I didn't learn about this until late. But I can get it for you tomorrow; and to show you I'm a man of my word, I've brought you this."

He pulled the envelope out of his inside coat pocket and set it on the counter. Tilman immediately picked it up and looked inside. "Three hundred? You bring me a lousy three hundred?"

"I'm sorry. It was all I could get. I swear it. Tomorrow I'll bring the rest."

For a moment Tilman just sat there slapping the envelope against his other hand. Then he shoved it into his own pocket.

"Okay. Tomorrow at noon. You be here."

"Yes."

"With the whole twenty thousand. I'm going to call this a bonus."

"But—yes." Albert got off his chair and almost fell. "Yes, all right. Is that all?"

"No." Tilman gestured to the brandy the bartender had placed on the counter. "Pay for your drink and don't be stingy with the tip. Vinnie's a friend of mine."

Albert reached into his pocket and then went from ghost white to ash gray. "You have all my money."

Tilman burst into laughter. "Go on, get out of

here, junior." As Albert all but ran for the door, he watched, shaking his head. "Jerk."

He drew a bill out of the envelope and set it out for the bartender, before taking Albert's brandy and gulping it down. Then he wiped his mouth with the back of his hand and looked at Rennie.

"Let's get out of here."

"But I haven't finished my drink."

"You don't need it. I'm gonna keep you plenty warm."

With that, he took her arm and directed her toward the door. Had Albert had enough time to get away? she wondered. Would Killian and his men be in position? She adjusted her purse and gripped it firmly, ready to reach for her gun if necessary.

Together they stepped into the artificially lit street.

"Which way?" Tilman asked.

Rennie gestured over her shoulder and they began to walk. They got only a few yards when a police car came around the corner with its siren blaring and lights flashing.

It hadn't been part of the plan.

As she reached for her gun, police sprang up from behind several cars. Tilman's reactions were better than most; he drew his own gun from his belt and jerked Rennie back against him. The motion sent her purse flying. It hit the sidewalk and the gun slipped out skidding farther.

"You're a cop," he whispered furiously.

"And you're surrounded," she managed, struggling against the choking band of his forearm against her throat.

"Tilman!" Killian shouted. "There's no way out of this. Let her go and put the gun down."

"Go to hell! I'm not going back behind bars. You try to take me and she gets it first. Now let me walk."

"You know we can't do that. Don't add murder to the charges already piled up against you."

"What have I got to lose?"

"Wait!" Nate pushed past Killian and elbowed his way onto the sidewalk. Despite the detective's angry directive for him to get back behind the car, he stepped closer to Tilman and raised his hands in surrender. "Let her go, Len, and take me instead."

"*Montgomery?*"

"Nate, go back!" Rennie cried.

"Let her go." He took a step closer. "She doesn't have anything to do with this. Take me."

"I ain't going to *take you*, Montgomery," Tilman snarled, shifting the gun to point it at him. "I'm going to get *rid* of you!"

"No!"

Rennie's scream tore into the night. Disregarding the stranglehold around her neck, she lunged at the arm with the gun. Grabbing Tilman's hand, she simultaneously pushed it up and away from his body seeking to break his hold by way of his thumb. But the motion sent them both off balance and, with her hands slipping over the revolver, the gun discharged.

Chapter Ten

Everything happened at once and in the center of it all was a searing pain burning through her hands. People surrounded them. Screaming, Tilman lunged at her. Hands appeared from every direction to draw them apart. Someone picked up Tilman's revolver; for a moment she stared at it not remembering it falling from her grasp. Then someone else was folding her into a fierce embrace and she realized it was the only thing that mattered now.

"Rennie...Rennie."

"That was a damned foolish thing to do, counselor," she said, her voice sounding strangely flat even to her own ears.

"Look who's talking...Rambo, Jr."

"I think you're both nuts," Killian said, joining them. But there was a hint of a smile on his face. Having collected Rennie's gun and her purse, he offered them to her.

She gave him a dry look.

He dropped his own gaze to her hands. "Let me see 'em," he sighed.

"See what?" Nate demanded.

"I'm okay," Rennie hedged.

Killian grunted. "Take a look at her hands. When she fell with Tilman, her hands slipped. They were on the revolver when it went off."

"Let me see." Nate adjusted his hold of her by grasping both of her wrists and turning her palms upright, exposing the black streaks that permeated torn skin.

"Powder burns," Killian explained. "She took the full blow, all right. By the way," he added to Rennie, "it might make the pain more worthwhile if you know that you broke his thumb."

"I'd be happier if you said it was the fall that did that. As crazy as he is, he'll probably try to sue me for assault."

"He's not going to be suing anybody. A parolee in the possession of a Saturday night special, repeating the crime he was originally convicted for? He's going to be too busy serving time."

Staring at her hands, Nate's expression turned

murderous. He made a move toward the group where policemen were handcuffing Tilman and reading him his rights. Without thinking, Rennie reached for him, winced, and readjusted her hold. "It was my fault—and it's over."

Nate hesitated a moment longer before relenting. "All right, but we're getting you to the hospital."

"What for? I can clean this up myself."

"Those burns are pretty bad," Killian said, shaking his head. "I think you'd better let a doctor have a look at you. Besides, the public is beginning to crawl out from behind the woodwork and, before you know it, the media will be here, too. Unless you want to be on the morning news, I suggest you get out of here." He signaled a patrolman. "He'll take you to emergency and then drive you home."

"Excuse me...could we catch a lift with you?" Faith asked. She and Albert had been standing quietly to the side, and now edged toward them.

Rennie could sense Nate about to reject the idea. "Of course," she said quickly. "You'll want to be with Maggie, won't you? I'm sure she's already worrying about you. Nate, if you'd take my purse for me, we can leave."

The ride to the hospital took only minutes but was made in total silence. Once there Nate tried to rush Rennie inside, but she held back to speak to Faith.

"I hope things work out for you," she told her. "And I want you to know I'm sorry for having to deceive you. But—I do care."

Faith glanced over to where her husband stood awkwardly watching Nate speak to the patrolman. "I know he doesn't have Nate's dashing looks, nor your bravery; but he had the courage to stand up to his father, and I'm very proud of him for that."

"I wouldn't say he wasn't brave; you should have seen him in that bar. He was perfect."

"Really?" Faith's face brightened with pride and love a moment before guiltily eyeing Rennie's hands. "You were the one who took the biggest risks."

"Maybe," she sighed, catching Nate's eye. "But it wasn't anything I wouldn't do again."

"Yes, I can see that. Good luck to you."

As Faith and Albert went inside and headed for the elevators, Nate took Rennie into emergency. Before he had a chance to say anything to her, she was being led away by a young intern.

Again reduced to waiting, he thought morosely. For the first time he took notice of the other people lining the hallway and sitting on the plastic-and-chrome chairs. Old and young alike, they all held the same expressions—bewilderment, anxiety. Not all of them were likely to hear good news by the time the waiting was over. At least he had that working in his favor. He had the comfort of knowing he had another chance.

He had a lot to be thankful for, he reminded himself, settling down on the chair farthest from everyone else. Yet he'd been greedy, hadn't he? He'd waited a long time to find the woman he wanted to spend the rest of his life with. Yet he'd been trying to mold Rennie into something else from the moment he began to pay attention to dangers she faced in her work. That she should be a private detective was hardly something he would have wished for, but did it give him the right to ask her to give up her work because he didn't like it? If he wanted her, wanted *them* to have a chance together, didn't he owe it to her to try to let her fulfill her needs? If that meant continuing in the profession she'd been raised into, then so be it. After all, when he considered his options, was any other choice bearable?

"That should fix you up," the smiling doctor said, securing the last strip of gauze. "Now all you have to worry about is remembering to keep these out from under water taps."

Rennie held up her bandaged hands. "I feel like a mummy."

"I get off in about thirty minutes. Do you need someone to take you home? This kind of injury can be tough when you're trying to fit keys into locks and stuff."

And stuff? Rennie smiled. "Thanks for the offer, but there's someone outside waiting for me."

"The Heathcliff look-alike I saw when I turned your forms in to the cashier?" When he saw Rennie's eyes begin to sparkle, he playfully clutched his heart and stumbled for the door. "I'll send him in."

Rennie's smile faded the moment the door closed behind him. Okay, she thought, suddenly gripped by a case of nerves. This is it. There's no more case and no more excuses. It's total honesty time. Don't be a coward and blow it again.

"Hi."

She looked up from the green tiled floor and saw him standing hesitantly at the door. "Hi."

Dear God, he looks good, she thought. She wanted to throw herself into his arms and kiss away the lines of strain she saw lingering on his face. Instead she lifted her hands and shrugged.

"Guess my goose is cooked for a while."

"Does it hurt?"

"Not really."

He took a step closer. She drew her lower lip between her teeth.

"Rennie, I—"

"Nate—"

They laughed and she began to slide off the examining table, but stumbled. Nate grabbed her by her waist.

"I guess I'm—" She looked up and found herself drowning in his eyes. "Oh, Nate, hold me."

"Sweetheart." He drew her close and buried his face in her hair. "I can't hold this in any longer, Rennie. You might not be ready to hear this but—I love you."

"I love you, too."

Nate framed her face with his hands and stared at her, drinking in the truth shining in her eyes. Then he lowered his head and kissed her deeply.

"I won't stand in your way," he whispered against her lips.

"I've been thinking about it a lot lately."

"If your job makes you happy, I want you to keep it."

"The only decision I came to is that it *is* simply a job—and an empty replacement to being with you."

Nate lifted his head slightly. "Say that again?"

"Weren't you listening?" she teased. "I love you."

He slipped his hands deeper into her hair. "Marry me."

"Yes."

"Have my children."

"Oh, yes."

They kissed again, and laughed and planned until a nurse came in and gently threw them out. When they exited the hospital minutes later, they found the patrol car still waiting for them as promised.

"Will you file charges against Wendell?" Rennie asked, resting her head against Nate's shoulder.

"No. What's the purpose? The only ones who would really suffer are Maggie, Faith and Albert, and they've been through enough."

"Home, folks?" the patrolman asked, opening the back door for them.

"Can we make a small detour?" Nate asked, smiling down at Rennie. "There's someone at your place I think we need to pick up first."

Rennie laughed with delight. "Darling, you don't know what you're letting yourself in for, but I love you."

"Just don't ever stop," he told her and helped her into the car.

Farther down the driveway, out of reach of the brightly lit entryway, a black stretch limousine waited. Inside, an elegantly dressed man sat back and smiled.

"Can we go home now, boss?" Rocco asked from the front seat.

"*Si*, now we can go home. But tomorrow you remind me to wire my brother in Palermo, eh? I think we'll send vino for the wedding."

Rocco rolled his eyes. "Yes, sir, Mr. De-Palma."

Moments after the patrol car drove away, the limousine did, too.

* * * * *

WAYS TO *UNEXPECTEDLY* MEET MR. RIGHT:

♡ *Go out with the sexy-sounding stranger your daughter secretly set you up with through a personal ad.*

♡ *RSVP yes to a wedding invitation—soon it might be your turn to say "I do!"*

♡ *Receive a marriage proposal by mail—from a man you've never met....*

These are just a few of the unexpected ways that written communication leads to love in Silhouette *Yours Truly.*

Each month, look for two fast-paced, fun and flirtatious *Yours Truly* novels (with entertaining treats and sneak previews in the back pages) by some of your favorite authors—and some who are sure to become favorites.

YOURS TRULY™:
Love—when you least expect it!

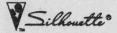

SILHOUETTE®

Desire®

Do you want...

Dangerously handsome heroes

Evocative, everlasting love stories

Sizzling and tantalizing sensuality

Incredibly sexy miniseries like **MAN OF THE MONTH**

Red-hot romance

Enticing entertainment that can't be beat!

You'll find all of this, and much *more* each and every month in **SILHOUETTE DESIRE**. Don't miss these unforgettable love stories by some of romance's hottest authors. Silhouette Desire—where your fantasies will always come true....

▼ *Silhouette* ROMANCE™

What's a single dad to do when he needs a wife by next Thursday?

Who's a confirmed bachelor to call when he finds a baby on his doorstep?

How does a plain Jane in love with her gorgeous boss get him to notice her?

From classic love stories to romantic comedies to emotional heart tuggers, **Silhouette Romance** offers six irresistible novels every month by some of your favorite authors! Such as…beloved bestsellers **Diana Palmer, Annette Broadrick, Suzanne Carey, Elizabeth August** and **Marie Ferrarella,** to name just a few—and some sure to become favorites!

Fabulous Fathers…Bundles of Joy…Miniseries… Months of blushing brides and convenient weddings… Holiday celebrations… You'll find all this and much more in **Silhouette Romance**—always emotional, always enjoyable, always about love!

SR-GEN

FIVE UNIQUE SERIES
FOR EVERY WOMAN YOU ARE...

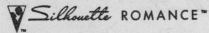 ROMANCE™

From classic love stories to romantic comedies to emotional heart tuggers, Silhouette Romance is sometimes sweet, sometimes sassy—and always enjoyable! Romance—the way you always knew it could be.

Red-hot is what we've got! Sparkling, scintillating, *sensuous* love stories. Once you pick up one you won't be able to put it down...only in Silhouette Desire.

Silhouette ® SPECIAL EDITION ®

Stories of love and life, these powerful novels are tales that you can identify with—romances with "something special" added in! Silhouette Special Edition is entertainment for the heart.

SILHOUETTE·INTIMATE·MOMENTS®

Enter a world where passions run hot and excitement is always high. Dramatic, larger than life and always compelling—Silhouette Intimate Moments provides captivating romance to cherish forever.

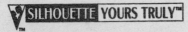 YOURS TRULY™

A personal ad, a "Dear John" letter, a wedding invitation... Just a few of the ways that written communication unexpectedly leads Miss Unmarried to Mr. "I Do" in Yours Truly novels...in the most fun, fast-paced and flirtatious style!

SGENERIC-R1